AFRICAN WRITERS SERIES

Editorial Adviser · Chinua Achebe

22

THE SECOND ROUND

AFRICAN WRITERS SERIES

Lenrie Peters

THE SECOND ROUND

HEINEMANN EDUCATIONAL BOOKS LTD
LONDON IBADAN NAIROBI

Heinemann Educational Books Ltd
48 Charles Street, London W1X 8AH
PMB 5205, Ibadan · POB 25080, Nairobi
EDINBURGH   MELBOURNE   TORONTO
SINGAPORE   HONG KONG   AUCKLAND

SBN 435 90022 6

Printed by St Paul's Press Ltd, Malta

To Rosemary

I

The city lies bemused
on a craggy coast
against the Atlantic
where elements fuse.
Purged by waterways
and howling wind
with deception of bell-tones
at the etiolated
unending confluence of patterns;
seated and cross-legged
but only half composed
like green leaves
on dying trees.

A glitter of rock salt
encircled by mountains
she tilts skyward,
seaward and skyward
arms stretched outward
in the sun drench
like some shore-washed monster
feeble at the lion's feet
for they are the Lion Mountains;
the Sierra Leone.

Poised at the diastolic
moment of change,
indignant at the deafening
clangour of contrasting possibilities
she sifts realities
at conscience beat;
Amaranthine in the crude
extravagance of her torment
where the sunset wades into the night
and colour on sparkling colour
of tense gaiety
sudden like the change of weather
seeps through her century
of broken passions and near forgotten hope
with the intangible flicker of perfume

But come what may
her every root and hope
lie in the cotton tree
which overlooks the bay.

II

The people are like the city.
The people are the city
come to life
with every subtle change of sundown light
who often fold their hands
over their heads
if not across their breasts.
Their tempers are volcanic and unearthed
but they are rich; so rich in beauty.

There you will see a smile
shimmer like an oasis
and a soul-bound gesture; innocent,
pregnant like a heap of roses.

On Sundays they answer the tolling of bells
cling clanging from Goderich to Kent
harnessed in Harris tweed and felt
with lusty voices broad as the Veldt,
the women like plumed chestnut in silver and gold.
But darkness is absence of light
and darkness enhances light.
The people of the city are velvet dark
they blossom at moonfall.

III

Two seasons alternate
the wet heat and the dry
Ocean breeze desert wind
plough up what they can find;
The people's thoughts are no less protean.

Where energy belongs to nature
God help the human creature
When Homo runs the show
God help Himself.

Their habits and attitudes
ferment between extreme polarities
God has not had an airing
since the anti-slavery laws were passed.

Recreated every Sunday
lavishly entombed on weekdays
because for ready action
there's no better than the devil.
The after life is all very well
but how about the here and now? by hell!
Daddy Sori, uncle John
Mamma Akosua, Kanimpon
Cockle shell, pigeon droppings
all play their part
when it comes to succeeding.

IV

The city is old and worn
uncoordinated, but full of fun
like her close friend the sun.
She keeps beaming
to seaward leaning
attentive to strange echoes
with a wrinkle and a smile
that imperishable glint in her eye; –
sea drums documenting the future
and every strained moment
which shivers, cracks and blasts in tomorrow.

Every now and then
her indulgent heart is rocked
by new vistas
parcelled in pressurized time
and she moves an inch or two,
nods recognition to me and you.

x

After the cloud and rain
the sun always shines again.

The city is like any other, but free.
The city is Freetown
from Kroo Bay to Cline Town
Brookfields to Fourah Bay
Free as a summer cloud
and inordinately proud.

Chapter One

It was a warm July day when Dr Kawa arrived home from England. An angry day with the sea rough and demoniacal and there was no harmony between the steady frankness of the sun and the dark raging horrors of the water. A testing but familiar day to the people of Freetown.

Across the bay, from the quay of white reinforced concrete recently built to cope with the increasing trade of the territory, the Lunga coast shimmered into a mere translucence through the spray of the waves and the eye-stinging dryness of the air. Undaunted, a few smoke-belching launches heaved ineffectually through the waves and the hardy canoe boys still carved their way out to unload the smaller ships which could not come alongside the quay.

Crowds of relatives, friends and loafers had arrived on the quay to welcome the passengers by the time the *Accra* docked at 11 a.m., her flags flying and her double blast greeted by loud cheers from the crowd. Groups of women in colourful cotton prints and intricate head-ties seemed to hold their breath as the liner side-stepped gracefully alongside. Hardly were her ropes secure than there burst out a spontaneous and progressive exchange of thrown kisses, fluttering handkerchiefs and wild gesticulations between the passengers on deck and the welcoming parties. In a moment the crowd had become so animated that everyone was completely absorbed into the warmth of welcoming.

Mr Marshall moved away from the edge of the quay where the waves rose so high that he was covered in salt spray, and joined the body of the crowd. He was a tall, light-skinned man, easy in his movements, who looked older than the early fifties of his years. His bald head was beaded with drops of sweat. As he moved slowly through the crowd the unnatural dryness of his countenance, the far-searching look in his eyes and his detachment were swept away by the joy and energy of the people round him. He, like many who knew none of the passengers, threw in his weight with those who did, and shouted out the name which was being most vociferously chanted next to him; a name which could have belonged to any of the hundreds of passengers or could have been entirely fictitious. It was an opportunity for merry-making, not often ignored in Africa, and any name was good enough.

A plump woman waving a silk handkerchief behind him dug her elbow into his spine and apologized. He looked round into the powdered creases of her armpit along which rivulets of sweat were beginning to eat their way. She had an open childlike face and laughed with un-restrained fullness.

'They say Dr Kawa is coming home at last,' she began.

'I don't know him,' Mr Marshall said.

'Ah! I don't know him too, but I have heard so much about him that I decided to come and welcome him,' she replied, as if Mr Marshall's statement was irrelevant.

'What is he "doctor" of?'

'Medicine; and I hear he has specialized in women's

affairs,' she said with pride, and followed this with a naughty giggle.

'One never knows these days, what with everyone coming back from the States as a doctor of something or other,' Mr Marshall said seriously. This moved her to floods of laughter and, unable to contain herself, she laid a hand on his near shoulder, holding her side with the other. He felt oddly stirred by the fine strands of 'chewing-stick' which lodged between her teeth.

'Look! Look! There is Rebecca; Lord 'ave mercy; Rebecca!!' screamed a small woman who was standing on her toes the better to expose herself to Rebecca; unfortunately in her excitement she only fell over each time she tried. Those around her followed the pointing finger to where a tall girl in slacks stood on the lower deck. A number of voices sang 'Rebecca' and succeeded in attracting her attention. But the little woman, almost paralysed with emotion, still could not make herself seen. Mr Marshall, seizing her by the waist, lifted her above the heads in front so that she was able to embrace Rebecca from across the distance.

'Doesn't she look wonderful well?' she asked as he put her down. He agreed.

'She is my niece, you know.' He said he did not know.

'Yes, I brought her up since she was so high,' she told him spreading her hand out waist-high.

'Her mother died tragically when she was only a child and I had to look after her.' She paused and added with feeling and pride, 'She's been studying in England you know. Won a scholarship.'

'Nice! Is that where she is coming from now?' asked the plump woman.

'This boat doesn't come from anywhere else,' the small woman replied, a little hurt by the question.

3

'I was only askin',' the other said defensively.

'Why aren't you going on board to meet her?' Mr Marshall asked.

'Hum. You are right to ask. It isn't every day that a daughter comes home from England. But you think it's easy to go on board? Don't you know you have to get a ticket?' She looked up suddenly into Mr Marshall's eyes and added 'Sir?'

'I know, but you only have to apply for one,' he said.

'Apply? You don't live in this country, sir. You don't know you have to shake hand before they will even promise you one? Then when you finally get the ticket you have to bribe again.' She spoke with agitation and sadness.

'Is it as bad as that?' Mr Marshall asked absent-mindedly.

'Oh yes, and in these hard times I don't even have enough to feed my old mother, let alone "shaking hands" everywhere with officials.' She smiled to indicate she bore no malice.

'Do you know which one is Dr Kawa?' the plump woman asked.

'You mean *the* Dr Kawa?'

'Yes; I hear he is coming home on this boat.'

The small woman gave a slow sarcastic chuckle. 'He's lost for good. He's never coming home again. Likes the English winter or the women, I don't know which. We gave him up a long time ago.' This she said with a backward wave of the hand which conveyed the finality of the grave.

'But I heard from a very reliable source that he was on this boat,' the plump woman insisted.

'I'm sorry; you must have got the names mixed up. And he is a scholarship boy as well – it was after the

4

Government could not get him to come home after his training that they insisted on all scholarship holders signing a bond to say they will return immediately after qualifying.'

'You are sure?' the other asked disappointedly.

'You can wait an' see if you don't believe me,' the small woman said, returning her attention to Rebecca.

'Why wouldn't he come home?' Mr Marshall asked.

'Said the Government did not offer him enough money – after they had paid for his education. After Independence, all right; we shall have enough money to pay anything we like. But now —' She broke off abruptly and strained her neck to find Rebecca again, but she had left the deck. Her eyes wandered along the upper deck, stopped and concentrated their gaze.

'Lord 'ave mercy – wonders will never cease,' she intoned in a hushed voice, shielding her mouth in a gesture of surprise.

'There is Dr Kawa.'

The plump woman assaulted Mr Marshall again in her excitement.

'Which one? Where?' she shouted elbowing shoulders out of her way as if her life depended on seeing Dr Kawa.

'I told you,' she murmured. 'I told you I 'eard 'e was on the boat, from a very reliable source.'

'Up there . . . with the dark glasses,' the small woman pointed.

'Dat one? Dat one there wit de khaki trousers and de cap?' the plump woman asked when she had recovered her breath. 'Is dat what all de talk is about? Dr Kawa. Dr Kawa. To my mother, I thought 'e was a real man.'

'Did you expect a film star?' the small woman asked. The plump woman, disappointed, sulked and wiped her face and dripping armpits recklessly with her silk handkerchief.

She looked around her, wishing to withdraw. But the gangway was being lowered and the crowd pressed forward. Courageously the plump woman rode the current and as she was lifted forward searched in vain for some other figure on whom she could lavish her adulation.

Dr Kawa did not seem anxious to disembark, as if his mind was still unmade. Mr Marshall took only a passing glance at him, but afterwards could remember the man apart, with his open-necked shirt and cloth cap a size too large.

Soon the passengers were hurrying down the steps, their arms laden with parcels, the women clutching their hats. Somewhere in the background a group broke out singing and danced to the throbbing of drums. The tall waves lashed the shore, the passengers threw themselves breathlessly into the arms of friends and relatives. The sun seemed to shut an eye.

One unfortunate woman caught her pointed heel on the very last step and pitched forward scattering her parcels over the quay. As she screamed her dentures fell into the sea. The crowd howled with innocent zest. The rumour spread that she had found a dentist in London who had been willing to extract her perfectly good set of teeth because she had thought dentures were the fashion.

Mr Marshall forced his way out of the crowd feeling relieved from the pressure of his private thoughts by the music and dancing around him. He felt the joy of life and affection forced upon him and he was powerless to reject it.

As he reached his car he saw a boy going through the Goods Exit.

'Hey you! Where you think you're going? You don't hear? I said wha your pass?' The customs guard caught up with the boy and challenged him, his menacing truncheon raised high above his head. The boy turned and faced the guard.

'You pass. Who you think you har . . . dammit. You don't hear I call for you pass?' he shouted.

'Which pass?' the boy asked automatically.

'You pass to leave the wharf.'

'I got in without one.'

'Don't matter how you get in. Must 'ave one to go h'out.'

'Where can I get a pass?' the boy asked the truncheon.

'Back through Customs, turn left. When you reach Number 2 shed is a window. Request dere for a ticket and bring ticket to me.'

'Yes,' the boy said, resuming his steps back through the gate.

'Bloody hell!' the guard shouted as the boy put the iron fence between them.

The boy returned a derisive look which the guard mistook for an apology.

'Ticket man gone to lunch till Monday morning,' he shouted helpfully.

Mr Marshall beckoned to the boy and offered him a lift home.

It was one o'clock and the sirens, war legacies, began to whine. A clamour rose into the air as invisible workmen everywhere laid down their tools for the week-end.

Mr Marshall and the boy drove through the goods entrance, saluted by the bureaucratic keeper of the gate, and on through the deserted Saturday afternoon streets of Cline Town.

Chapter Two

The Kawas lived in a modest house on Charles Street opposite the Boys' High School. The walls were of timber painted a reddish brown colour, the roof was aluminium and there was a porch for taking the air on warm evenings.

Mrs Kawa had stayed awake through the previous night tossing in bed restlessly and accompanying the chimes of the clock with sobs. Even she had despaired of ever seeing her only son again. Long before the Rhode Island cock had decided to wake the neighbours Mrs Kawa was up, arranging and attending to a thousand necessities. Though nervous with expectation she went about it methodically and unhurriedly. The family photographs which were put away at her husband's death were again hung round the walls with their venerated collection of dust and cobwebs, just as they had been before her son left home.

Mrs Kawa had decided on a grand welcome for her son if it was the very last thing she did, and as he had specifically asked to be spared the traditional welcome on disembarkation she had planned his reception at home. It was what her husband would have wished. No one was going to point a finger at her for stinting. The house was accordingly amply filled with food and drink. The scent

8

of flowers on the tables helped the flavour from the heavily spiced mounds of cooked mutton, poultry and rice to intoxicate the guests. The drummers and dancers had arrived early and, squatting on the sand in the yard, had been warming their throats and drums for hours. Only one slight hitch had occurred during the course of the morning when the Principal of the school had protested against the 'rowdy palaver' of the celebrations At this insult Mrs Kawa, who had never said an angry word in her life, thrust her head out of the window to hear the school singing *Rule Britannia!* and had told him to mind his own business.

She had moved her own things out of the only large bedroom kept cool by window shutters and made homely with the aroma of medicinal potions, ginger and liniment. She had set the pillow in the middle of the brass-limbed bed with the mosquito net neatly drawn back. 'I shall sleep in the small bedroom,' she had mused with tender satisfaction.

As the taxi rounded the corner of Charles Street the 'look-outs' gave the signal and the drummers struck out, moving in rhythm towards the gate, each cadence from the drums punctuated by an ecstatic nasal shriek from the master drummer.

Mrs Kawa hurried to her favourite chair at the end of the corridor facing the door and wiped away a furtive tear. There Dr Kawa had often sat on her knee as a boy and heard the family history handed down – all except the unmentionable interlude of the Slave Trade. In her excitement she could not find either a comfortable or natural position. First she folded her arms across her chest and decided it looked too sombre. Then she rested them on the arms of her chair and thought this attitude lacked warmth. Her heart was beating so quickly that she felt she could not trust it not to leap clean out of her chest. Meanwhile she chewed a green pepper to calm her nerves and keep her blood pressure where it ought to be.

When Dr Kawa walked through the door she thought she would faint with joy, but she managed to get up from her chair, her arms spread out and her head tilted to one side. She observed him keenly and lovingly as he walked towards her, noting every mark of change in his eyes, his walk, even his thoughts. Murmuring a prayer with her eyes closed she flung herself at him and held his head to her breast for a consummate moment of happiness. Then with tears rolling freely down her face she released him to the crowd of well-wishers who had swarmed in like locusts ready and able to devour the new crop.

Dr Kawa was overwhelmed by the welcome and embarrassed by the open show of affection and subtle indictment in the way he was greeted.

'You have been away a long time,' one said.

'Now I have seen you again I can die in peace,' another.

In the midst of the rejoicing he felt slightly irritated because he could not measure up to the warm-heartedness around him nor find suitable words in reply. Mrs Kawa, recognizing his difficulty, proudly led the singing of a hymn in thanksgiving.

'Amen!' shouted an old man who had already armed himself with a bottle of lager and was searching for an opener.

'God has sent him back to oss, and we are grr-ateful,' responded a wiry old woman, sensing the moment of ecstasy approaching.

'And God said, for he was lost and is found. Kill the fatted calf, bo!' recited a younger man as he made his way towards the bottles at the other end of the room. Each outburst drew a conducted sigh from the company while the school bell from across the street added its timorous assent. There was joy and friendship, music and laughter.

Mrs Kawa indeed killed the fatted calf. She kept open house for a week, feasting all who came. Habitual spongers practically took up residence at the little house, systematically mopping up the drink. When finally the barrel ran dry, contented belches were to be heard all over Freetown. This was the signal for the old Mammies to invade the Kawa residence.

These dear rheumatoids arrived in twos and threes with the perspicacity of vultures descending on the ripped-open carcass of a deer; but though scavengers they looked, they were as clear-minded and extortionate as any Lebanese trader. Some knew the address, some had to be led to it, but all arrived.

They blessed Dr Kawa, admired his patriotism and he in return warmed their shaking hands with neatly-folded currency. They thanked him for the unexpected blessing from God, but as they could not break into his gift before they had prayed for him in the darkness of their own bedrooms, could he find it in his heart to add their return bus fares to it? Which he did.

If it was an expensive welcome which he could only have avoided by remaining in England, nevertheless it served as a useful investment and an infallible advertising campaign. Even before he had begun to lay his professional hand on the community, the rumour had spread that he was the best doctor Freetown had seen for many years.

Unfortunately for him, the rush of welcomers had scarcely slackened when the traditional end-of-the-month calls fell due, and, while the former depended on his good-will and sentiment, the latter involved a strict call to duty.

The marauders told him that everything about him, his

generosity, yes! especially his generosity, his affability and kind eyes had convinced them that all his years away from home in that hard and bitter country of Europe had not deprived him of his respect and understanding for their ancient customs. They were moved to tears because he had not forgotten any single one of them. They who had nursed him as a boy and watched him grow up until the day when, God willing, he had put on his first pair of full-length trousers. They who had prevented his exasperated father – of dear memory – from throwing his son through the windows on those nights when as a baby in arms, he would keep everybody awake with his crying. What heavenly memories returned to them as clearly as if they were incidents of yesterday. His kindness to them – slaves who had done no more than their duty and deserved only as much. All this they said, with eyes darting from the wonder of his face to that of the sky.

Only, they went on, old as they were, they were forced to look after a grandson whose father – the good-for-nothing – had taken to drink. The child had not been to school for a whole week because the fees had not been paid. They were only too aware of his – Dr Kawa's – responsibilities as the only man in his family and were deeply ashamed to add to them, but if he could find it in his heart – that heart which after all they had helped to nurture – if he could search in his pockets for a few shillings, they would continue to pray for him as they had always done. He obliged.

Only, for years the rain had come through the roof and the constant dampness accounted for their rheumatism. If he did not believe them he could go to see for himself, and they took his hand. But Mr Y out of sheer kindness had offered to put the roof right for next to nothing, and if Dr Kawa could find it in . . .

All things considered, while his reputation during those first weeks at home expanded, his finances began to show a startling decline, and matters were not helped when his mother presented him with a bill for £60 at the end of his first fortnight, as part of his welcoming expenses.

Gradually he overcame his amusement and then his irritation at the demonstrative and inquisitive temperaments which swarmed around him and who considered every moment of his life as equally their own. Slowly he began to feel at home and relaxed, looking forward to the spiced meals, and no longer feeling embarrassed by the constant sweating. The leisurely meandering life of the tropics struck him as the right tempo for the human body and the endless gyrations of human pursuits in colder climates as artificial and contrary to the laws of nature.

These thoughts came to him usually in the evenings when he sat in the half-light of the porch by the window overlooking the street, and he felt tempted to accept this ultimate simplicity of life unquestioningly. He would sit back, resting his shoulders and his brain. Thus to revitalize his nerves and let the fat roll over his body proved a great temptation. At those moments he would sit suddenly upright in his chair and recall his noble ideas about progress in Africa, would ask himself whether the sunshine was more intoxicating even than the alcohol. Like an addict he would resolve his conflict with a quick squirt into his veins of the hormone for the preservation of Western Man – 'feverish activity at all times' – and would go out for a walk down the boggy red earth trenches of Kroo Bay in the sweet stench of Slum Island, listening to the tuberculous chokings which poured out of the tin shacks. There he would watch the children with leg ulcers crack bloated lice between their finger-nails with the swift snap of horse-whips, while their mothers emptied dysentery pails into the uncomplaining waters of the bay. Along the back streets, through the nauseating din of flies and on to the main roads flanked by elegant air-conditioned houses, he would walk, asking himself what was responsible for that transformation from squalor and disease, ignorant superstition and degradation down by the bay, into the physical comforts of modern Freetown. If science – data and proof – had achieved this, then what did he dislike about it? about say, the motor-car? – nice comfortable shining time-saver. Was it its dehumanizing effect? The unsmiling dead hippopotamus look on the drivers' faces, the intolerable arrogance, the blindness and the greed? Once you had, for instance, a car, an endless line of scientific necessities stretched out and beckoned you into the distance. He remembered what a young barrister had told him: 'Take me for instance: I got a car on credit the moment I got back; then a refrigerator. But you can't just keep eggs in the fridge, you need booze. But what's the good of it all if you can't show it off! So you have a few friends in. Heavens above, I haven't got a house! Let's see; I could borrow – everybody borrows nowadays, even the Government lives by credit. But if you borrow you have to pay interest to a chap who doesn't mind how he makes his money. I must have gone soft in the head – plain monkey mad. It's naïve to think you can build an honest house these days. They tell me everyone takes bribes these days; everyone, even bishops and judges. You can bribe your way to heaven as quickly as spit out a hot potato. Who am I to try to carry the social conscience on my back anyway? One day some great social pioneer will turn up and straighten things out. He's bound to turn up sooner or later – things can't just go to the dogs. As for me I'm human and I'm only concerned with making my cell nice and padded any way I can. Another thing; when I get my new house I must find a nice progressive woman.'

That was it: squeeze out a man's personality like an orange pip and leave a whole lot of moving carcasses in splendid fall-out shelters.

Depressed by his attempt to isolate the links which so skilfully bound physical squalor to fertility of soil on the one hand, and the elegant shrouds of prosperity to barrenness on the other, he would find himself at the hospital. His nostrils dilated; he sniffed the air in search of that comfort which he hoped to find in the true harmony of science with human consciousness and fertility. Alas! they had not heard of science at the hospital. Medicine was still a hit or miss game with tons of luck thrown in, and any revolutionary upstart was merely heading for an early grave. The witch-doctor had been at it since the days of the cannibal and was thought quite adequate for most African needs.

Faced with frustrations, Dr Kawa wondered whether stagnation in any field that seemed potentially valuable was a reflection of the British genius for making their colonial peoples march no nearer than a century behind them, so that when frock coats and bowlers were being frowned on and discarded at Westminster, they had become the height of fashion in the tropical heat; or whether it was a cunning device of science to check its own overgrowth? Probably it was nothing more than a manifestation in social change of what biologists described as 'The ontology retracing the phylogeny.'

But his dispiriting thoughts did not then drive him to the depths of despair and depression which were to follow. Those were the painful days of readjustment, and, leaning against the once infallible pillar of reason, he continued to snarl out his questions. Where was the reconstruction to begin? What man could copy those ingenious wasps by thrusting his sting into the nerve centre of confusion without poisoning the entire system and say; 'That is where sickness begins; these are the very earliest beginnings of decay – this cloudy swelling' without being subjected to the humiliation of being put away safely, Christlike, on a shelf? But the body needed a certain minimum of organs to survive, and Jung had warned against stealing from people, even their neuroses, unless one had something better to put in their place. But sickness was one thing, a moral epidemic quite another.

One evening as he walked home from one of his impulsive walks with bowed head, his hands behind his back, he felt breathtakingly elated because he thought he had found the answer to some of his questions. It was an answer that would need a lot of pruning and reshaping and explaining, but an answer nevertheless – a starting point. He became overwhelmingly convinced that the trouble with the society into which he was snuggling like a roosting hen, was its weightlessness. Not light enough to take wings and soar but at the same time not heavy enough to settle on a firm foundation. A people at the middle way; the turning point. Hovering like evil ghosts and restless enough to be confused. He saw with an intuitive comprehension through the smiling faces and the rantings of the politicians the one collective visage of a frightened people. Frightened as if they had suddenly found themselves on the moon. People were always frightened. Frightened of pain, disease, love and death, but most of all frightened of emptiness, not knowing what they were about. So frightened in fact that they gave up trying to put things right and pretended nothing was the matter. Again the woman philosopher raised her intuitive head with shouts of 'If we are to die, then let's die screaming.'

Europe was frightened because she too was at the middle way and could not see round the corner. The whole world was frightened. Not so much of science or of nuclear bombs. The fear was deep inside the spirit of Man. If Mephistophelean science should win the wager, then his soul was gone – and there was only deluge, chaos, worse than chaos. So the blind had finally abandoned the blind – each for himself. The problem was not unique to Africa; it was only in a different shade of black. What was different was that Africa had a chance to stem it. Perhaps a last chance to banish the fear.

His mind turned to the origin of this fear. Was it conceit? Was it that man no longer felt the need to keep his feet warm in the milky bosom of the earth? Was it in his isolation from the harmony that held the earth to the sun and yet prevented the moon crashing into it? Here was a great event – the crystallization of vast energies into a mind, a perception able to understand and perhaps to throw back some little influence into the expanding whole. An organism which in a relatively short space of time had attained a position of dominance over the psychic impulse. What enormous opportunities opened to man and the universe for a happy remarriage between these opposing aspects of a fundamental reality. But rather like the centriole in the nucleus of a living cell at the moment of its dividing, at the very moment of its creation of new life through a process of sharing, they had positioned themselves at opposite poles and were held together precariously only by the flimsy threads of the artefactual spindle.

Worse still; time, which had appeared to be a fixed

corridor along which we might hurry into a distant nothingness, had suddenly shown itself to be indecently elusive. Since it was not running out on us, we had to put up with our own nasty work – not a pleasant thought. What a dilemma! Knowledge against self-disintegration. With luck we might bounce on to the next stage of evolution without memory of the past, not as men, but as morons perhaps. Something capable of living by the dictates of machines. *Progress!*

Chapter Three

Dr Kawa spent the first three weeks at his mother's, during which time she fed him on the health-giving foods which she said were missing from the cold salads and frozen meats of the English cuisine. Daily she prayed in thankfulness for his safe return and, while she was grateful to the English for giving her son knowledge and sophistication, she much lamented their neglect of his stomach. For his subdued temperament and tendency to reflection she had not decided on whom to lay the blame.

She would have liked him to stay longer with her so that she could more directly supervise his re-entry into the society, but Dr Kawa had already applied for a Government residence, and one morning a letter arrived informing him that his house was ready for occupation. To the letter a memorandum couched in intimate and seductive phrases was attached. It explained that provision was made whereby young recruits to the service could obtain loans from the Government. The stated priorities for which loans were available were the purchasing of a car, house, refrigerator and radiogram. Loans were repayable by monthly salary deductions at two and a half per cent interest.

'Never say no to anything the Government offers you,

boy,' Mrs Kawa had said on reading the memorandum. Initially Dr Kawa had resisted the temptation of increasing his indebtedness to the Government beyond the necessities of job and house, but soon discovered that his duties were so widely cast over city and peninsular that it was impossible to conduct his professional treasure-hunt without a car. He had faced the first compromise of his principle when he had gone back to the Government for the price of a car, and was shaken to observe that the monster was so impersonal that no loss of pride entered into the negotiations.

* * * * *

Mrs Kawa had gone with him to inspect the small red-brick bungalow which was to become his home; down the gravel drive between the croton hedges whose roots held the earth fractures together. The house was just off the main road with the playing fields of Brookfields in the background. To Mrs Kawa, who had crossed the threshhold blessing the house with a symbolic shower of spit, it had seemed a village church.

The furniture in the sitting-room was comfortable and unpretentious – a grey modern suite of three arm-chairs and a couch, with a polished teak dining table on which the dust had settled thickly. The bedroom was on the far side immediately opposite the front door and it led out into the lavatory and bathroom, a misarrangement which immediately caught Mrs Kawa's eye. The kitchen was diagonally across from the front door and opposite to that, a spare bedroom.

It was evening. Dr Kawa flung open a window and took in a deep breath. Because the hedge now sloped away he could see the large house next door set in cultivated surroundings.

'Who lives in that?' he asked.

'You don't want to bother your head about other people,' Mrs Kawa replied, too busy wandering round the room making a mental inventory of the furniture and filling in the blank spaces with what would be needed to make the place homely. The bare walls and floor did not please her.

'You'll need a carpet here for a start. These naked boards will get cold and damp when the September rains come down,' she said.

'Yes, but I shall need a few things to eat out of first.'

'That don't matter so. You can eat with me till you get properly settled. But you must have a carpet,' she insisted and she took a second turn around the room testing the windows for draughts.

'You'll need a houseboy and a woman to look after you – until you get married,' she commented, shrewdly observing his reactions.

'Can you trust me, a bachelor, with a woman?'

'The woman I have in mind will be safe enough.'

'I see, a chaperone.'

'Whatever that is, every home must have a woman,' Mrs Kawa said, smiling but with firmness in her voice.

'Even if she's just dropping into her grave?' Dr Kawa remarked facetiously.

'None of your flippancy. Grannie May is a good soul and will be proud to come and look after you. Have you forgotten how she used to pet and spoil you?'

'But there's no room. Where will they sleep?'

'I'd forgotten that,' she said thoughtfully with her index finger between her lips. 'Isn't it typical of the Government's thoughtlessness? How do they expect you to manage on your own? If it had been a European they . . .'

'But the last occupant was an Englishman. I met him,' Dr Kawa interrupted calmly.

'Well? didn't he have any servants?'

'Yes. He recommended his boy. But he did not live on the premises.'

'You're no wild Englishman trying to live like a savage. You must have a boy who lives here and can look after the house when you go out at night; be a sort of companion to you, till God willing you find a nice girl. They are scarce as good gold these days.'

'Of course if I built a small out-house he may agree to live in – the houseboy I mean – but that still doesn't settle Grannie May,' he said.

'Grannie May has her own home. But why should you build? Why shouldn't the Government build it? What will happen when you are sent up-country?'

Dr Kawa took her by the arm and together they walked round the room looking for architectural defects.

'We can't expect the Government to do everything for us you know,' he said at length. Mrs Kawa stopped dead, disengaging her arm.

'What have they done for us?' she asked and before he could reply she continued with growing agitation. 'Tell me what they have done for us – one – two – three – four. Tell me four good things they have done for us except keeping us backward and having a good time themselves?'

He stroked her shoulder affectionately and led her to a chair. He did not want to argue with her and knew how offended she would be if he did, yet he spoke out in spite of himself.

'Things are changing; every day. Ten years ago there wasn't a single African with real power, but now most of the power is in the hands of Africans. We can't go on singing the same old choruses, Mother.'

'But that is our birthright. This is our country. All right, tell me what they have done for us,' Mrs Kawa insisted.

'But we mustn't spend the next century moaning about what they have done and what they have not done for us. Perhaps it's just as well they haven't done too much. At least we shall have less to undo before we restart. We must get on with tackling the vital problems of Africa without making martyrs of ourselves. It's becoming a neurosis. I believe in Africa and I believe in the black man because he still has warmth left in him – the same warmth you and I borrow from the sun and transmit to the earth. He still has a smell so that when you go into his house you know a human being has been there. It is a kind of identity.'

He stopped suddenly, knowing that his preaching would be interpreted as an impertinence. He felt breathless and paralysed with loneliness. What was the good? How could one talk to a hypersensitive people about truth and real values when there was so much suspicion in their hearts, when every flower you offered was looked upon as a distraction from the fruits of material progress? How could you talk to a people who were looking for fire and brimstone? How could you stop them bolting down the poisoned apple offered from every quarter? He wanted to apologize to his mother, but he believed too strongly in what he had said to retract.

He felt immensely lonely: the loneliness of a child who lives on a beautiful estate with flowers and lawns, birds and an abundance of toys but with no one to play with.

He sat on the arm of a chair and sighed. To his feeling of loneliness was added remorse because he knew that his outburst was partly intended to divert his mother from the marriage theme on which she had begun, and she understood this. Since his return the marriage question had been broached so often by oblique and direct references that he was getting tired of it. People were beginning to make him feel abnormal.

Standing up awkwardly he flung his arms about apologetically. 'I'm sorry I raised my voice. You know how things build up inside you, and this happens to be something I feel strongly about. You promise to forget all I've said?'

Mrs Kawa did not promise to forget. Though she did not agree with everything he had said, she had been moved. She had stirred in her chair but decided it was not the time to spare him a rebuke. There would be battles ahead, and the hunter with only a few cartridges simply has to shoot straight.

'Don't forget, boy. We did not send you to England to lose your respect for your elders. I don't know what they do over there but in Africa we bring up our children to honour and love their parents.' She got up and made a final inspection of the room.

'Take me home now,' she said with pretended brusqueness.

Driving back in silence he realized how he had moved his mother and his loneliness left him.

*   *   *   *   *

Grannie May, though stooping with age, was agile for her eighty-six years and boasted of never having had to use spectacles to do the needlework which was her passion. Her arrival at the new house arranged by Mrs Kawa soon transformed it into a liveable-in and even cosy home. She swept the walls down and stood on a chair to reach the

24

spiders at the corners of the ceiling. She hung a few curios on the walls 'to make the place look homely', and stacked Dr Kawa's books away neatly in the glass-fronted bookcase which had belonged to his father and which his mother had insisted on his having: the large medical ones on the left and those in 'pepper-seed' print, as she called it, on the right. Cushions appeared on the chairs and two decorative mats covered the sitting-room floor until the ordered carpet should arrive. Grannie May had even stuck a few rose twigs into a patch of dry sand beside the house, away from the full glare of the July sun. Dr Kawa had politely but firmly resisted the introduction of a grey talking parrot to match the furniture and keep him company, but she had not consulted him when she had set up an earthenware kula (water jug) in one corner of the sitting-room with an enamel cup dangling from one of its spouts. She had thrown a seed or two of cola into the jug 'to sweeten the water' and when Dr Kawa had suggested that it might prove a breeding place for mosquitoes she had toddled off about her business without deigning to reply.

Her bird-like activity, her devotion and sternness, had so rekindled his boyhood fondness for her that he entered into the home-building with enthusiasm.

On her insistence he managed to get away from the hospital for a few hours one morning and called at Patterson Zochonis to get some cutlery and crockery, and remembered to buy the 'truth-telling mirror' which was a man's best friend and with whose honesty Grannie May had said that even she with her eighty-six years had not dispensed. At the store he had met an old school friend who had apparently been wafted into a cosy managerial job on the crest of a wave of Africanization of Government Departments and commercial interests.

They had embraced each other loudly and had talked of the old days, and when Dr Kawa had made his selection of silver and porcelain he had been told that it was not done for a professional person to deal in hard cash at a public store – all he had to do was to select whatever he liked and he, the sales manager, would arrange for a credit account. Dr Kawa had weakened and had been pressed with a bottle each of whisky and brandy. On his way back to the hospital he had stopped at Chanrai and had bought an exquisitely finished jade elephant for his bedside table, and Grannie May found room for it in her affections.

The houseboy had been engaged and had agreed to continue to sleep at home in Wilberforce until other arrangements could be made.

In one way and another his first weeks at the new home slid quickly by, and with his thoughts applied to practical considerations his mind had been free of the agonies of introspection. He had managed to visit his mother daily for however brief a stay. Often it had been restricted to a hurried kiss and an inquiry after her health. The clouds which had come between them had blown away and this helped to lighten his spirits.

*   *   *   *

One Saturday when Dr Kawa had worked late at the hospital he got home to find Grannie May dozing in a chair. As he was feeling tired himself and did not want a cooked supper, he insisted on her going home; but Grannie May would not hear of leaving before he had eaten to her satisfaction. He made a show of his determination by collapsing on to the couch and this disarmed Grannie May. With the air of someone who has been lured into a neglect of duty she slowly put her things together and left. He watched her go up the drive and she waved vaguely in his direction before her hurried steps took her out of sight.

Dr Kawa smiled at the irony of having spent so many years abroad training himself to domesticity, only to start reversing the process the moment he felt proficient. He took off his shoes and tie, sighed deeply and flung himself on the couch again. He was soon fast asleep.

It was dark when he awoke, and the clear night air was splintered only by the crickets protesting against the monstrous snorting of the toads. He searched for his cigarettes in the silvery light and lit one. The moonlight crept through the half-open window, fell across his body with a soothing caress and glittered on the floor. The complete relaxation of body and mind gave him a sensual satisfaction, the need of which he had not felt until that moment. Solitude suddenly seemed invaluable to him because he had recently had little time for reading or thinking in quietude. Enjoying every precious moment of the twinge the warm smoke gave him, he exhaled slowly and deliberately, watching the smoke glow in the mirror-glare of moonlight.

Episodes of his weeks at home returned to him in an analysable sequence and he decided that, all in all, things had not gone too badly; indeed he was enjoying being back more than he had dared to hope.

He mused over the quick substitution of his appetite for the burnt skeletons of the English autumn countryside into his love of the ruthlessness and dynamism of the African bush, and the human pathos which underlay the calm flow of conviviality. His work was going well and gave a great deal of satisfaction in spite of the frustrations and lapses in efficiency and the overpowering lethargy in some quarters. He felt the satisfaction of actually getting his teeth into things; but most of all he was gratified to think he was giving the community more than its prayer's worth of service. But still there was no room for smugness. There were bound to be many battles ahead, he told himself, and puffed out a smoke-ring.

Tender thoughts of his late father who had encouraged him to do the special course in obstetrics which was proving so valuable filled his mind.

'If you want to be a successful doctor, son, look after the women,' he had said in a whimsical mood, and Dr Kawa had not ignored the advice. A sudden pain of regret gnawed his chest because he had not returned home earlier during the years when his father was still alive and had weekly begged him to return, for now he felt it had been a weakness in his character. He and his father had always been close; how proud he would have been to see his son in the opening flower of success.

In the album of his memory he came across the page which had most enhanced his reputation during his weeks at home, and he lingered over it as he had done many times already.

It had been one of the many hectic days at the hospital when patients poured in like rain and flooded the place. He had been reminded of the accounts of human garbage in the Crimea. In the waiting-room was a mass of patients to be seen, while bulging into his consulting-room was the tail-end of those who had already been seen and were queuing outside the dispensary. Suddenly he had felt helpless and depressed, to relieve which he had decided to wander round the wards.

Outside the labour ward he had walked into the sister in charge. Confident, cheery and buxom, Sister Grace was familiar in her manner and harboured more than a trace of jealousy seasoned with contempt for the doctors.

'Where are you off to, this time of morning?' she had asked.

'Overwhelmed by the outpatient clinic. Anything doing up here?'

'Nothing much. Only a woman from the district who has been six hours in the second stage – brought in collapsed and shocked.'

'Why didn't you let me know, Sister?'

'Oh! There's nothing to be done for her. She's in there,' she had said off-handedly, resenting the tone of rebuke in his voice. Dr Kawa had been irritated by her attitude. It was true everybody was overworked, but he did not like the sisters taking upon themselves the full responsibility of deciding the prognoses of patients. But he was not in the mood for unravelling knotty problems that morning and his first impulse was to walk away and write a report to the matron about the attitude of the sisters which he considered bordered on negligence. Instead he had walked into the labour ward.

There he found a woman of about forty lying unconscious on a couch with a white sheet spread over her as if she were already dead. Pulling back the sheet and scarcely reasoning out the situation as was natural with him, he had known that she could be saved. She was pulseless and sweating and her pupils were fixed. There was no time to give her an anaesthetic or transfusion.

He picked up a sterilized knife and opened the abdomen. The foetus was lying free in the pelvis; the uterus torn from end to end. He removed the foetus and did what toilet he could, stitching the torn edges of the uterus together. Her recovery was a miracle.

Since leaving the hospital the woman had walked several miles unfailingly each week to leave a few eggs by his door, because she said that her life belonged to him.

The news of his prowess over this case had spread quickly and widely; misquoted, distorted, always exaggerated – it was said that the child also survived – and certain fastidious women refused to push during their confinements and uteri went on strike and would not contract, much to the mortification of the midwives, unless Dr Kawa was in attendance. But as there was a limit to the number of deliveries he could supervise personally, it would happen that one of his colleagues would be called in at the last moment to manage a reluctant uterus because Dr Kawa was not available, and the poor man would find himself landed with a stillbirth.

But once again the revolving thread of his thoughts began to slow down as he listened to the whisper of the dark silence, and soon he was in the kleptomaniac clutches of sleep. He had scarcely pulled the final blind over his consciousness when he was disturbed by a surreptitious tapping on the door. Opening his eyes and straining his ears he heard the banana limpness of a woman's knock repeated, and his breathing quickened with annoyance.

No, he would not answer the door! he fretted. Whoever it was would have to go away. People had to learn to respect his privacy; so he waited uncomfortably. Soon he was visualizing the long hours of siege with himself cramped on the couch while his tenacious caller stood guard outside, then how after a suitable interval he might steal to the window and peep out at the caller through the curtain only to find her waiting at the window. Anyway the north window was open and any moment a pair of eyes would be peering at him out of the darkness. Crying damnation he walked grudgingly to the door and switched on the light.

Outside were four middle-aged women whom he

had never seen before. Still not quite awake he stood
there and observed the quartet questioningly until one
spoke.

'Won't you ask us in, Doctor?' came the undisguised
sarcasm.

'I'm afraid I don't have surgery on Saturdays.'

'We are not patients,' the voice replied, almost forcing
an entry with its tone.

'Oh! I see,' he said as he swung the door open and in-
vited them in. They shook hands as they filed past.
The first was a small woman with qualities of leadership
who immediately looked round the room like a detective.
The second was twice her size. Dr Kawa offered each a
chair and sat in a straight-backed one himself facing them.
As they were busy appraising each item of furniture in the
room with critical glances, Dr Kawa crossed his legs and
felt content to wait.

'Nice house,' the large woman ventured, breaking the
silence.

'But so cold – ah! how do you manage to keep warm,
Doctor?' she added.

'Cold? Can I? W-would you like the window closed?'
he stammered with surprise, it being the middle of
summer.

'Don't worry about the window, Doctor,' the large
woman said as he got up to shut it.

'The height of summer . . .' he murmured sitting down.

'I know; but it takes a long time to reach the bones,'
she replied, showing signs of restlessness.

'We are sorry to disturb you,' the small woman said
firmly.

'Doctor, could you spare a glass of water?' the large
woman asked.

'Certainly,' said he, rising to fetch it when he noticed

the hurt look on the large woman's face and the meaning of her references became clear to him.

'Would you prefer some brandy?' he asked.

'As if we would refuse!' the large woman replied.

Brandy in hand, the warmth began to seep into the bones, and the barriers to disappear.

'How is the work, Doctor?' the small woman asked.

'Heavy, but enjoyable,' he said.

Mrs Coker (first left) sat bolt upright and properly in her chair with hands clasped demurely round the glass on her lap. She was small, well-proportioned and young for her sixty years. Her thin sharp lips emphasized the intelligence of her features but one felt that she would bite them viciously if she was upset. The cheek bones were high and prominent, and behind her wire-rimmed spectacles lurked the tension of someone who is deaf and is constantly afraid that jokes are being made at her expense.

She was a woman who did not make friends easily, and because of her reputation for frankness was always being pushed forward into a position of leadership which she did not strenuously resist, and which she had even come to assume by right. Other women admired her courage, despised her stoicism, yet it was always to her that they would turn when their husbands needed to be brought to heel. She could be relied upon to make a success of the assignment without turning things to her own advantage.

She came from a good family, unlike Miss Baker beside her whose ancestors had actually reached the cotton plantations of the deep South, and from nostalgia for the great open spaces they had preserved the wide-brimmed straw hats and apron skirts of the plantation fashions. But Mrs Coker's ancestors had been intercepted through the beneficence of Wilberforce and his supporters and had been left to stew together with Irish potatoes and a crowd of good-for-nothings from London prisons at a place called Freetown.

The population of Freetown had largely issued out of this many-coated collection. Some of the original settlers had migrated in dispirited bands towards the southern coasts in search of their ancestral graves, but most of them had accepted their new condition and had struggled to weave its incompatibilities into a tribal unit. Some had made good, and Mrs Coker's family was one of those. Over the years they had increased their power and education. Some, she claimed, had even shaken hands with Queen Victoria when they were given the mandate to go back and keep their people quiet and contented, with the help of a handful of European administrators. This pledge they never shirked, and considered themselves, and had in fact, become, the *élite* puppets over the tribal masses. Mrs Coker despised Miss Baker for having established contact with the New World through her past generations, and she could never forgive those she thought of as the 'lazy illiterate millions up-country'. With that inversion of moral judgement which exculpates the oppressor and derides the oppressed, Mrs Coker keenly scorned their lack of adventurous spirit.

At a time when Miss Baker's ancestors had succumbed to the mixtures of rum and sucrose on warm sandy beaches and had been herded half-way across the Atlantic senseless with drink and diarrhoea in the cold bellies of sailing ships, Mrs Coker's ancestors had turned their thoughts to polygamy. Yet she was conscious that but for the timely and historic intervention of Wilberforce, she would have been a 'Miss Baker'. But in those days people did not look for self-interest in every act of faith. Strengthened by tradition, she had always extended willingly to the millions up-country the missionary hand which kept them on their knees.

Miss Baker (second left) was not a small woman, and the warmth of her personality sprang from a heart proportionately large. There were deep rings in the flesh round her neck which made it appear dislocated and her brown eyes had the solemn and disarming quality of a deer's. The hands were large and loving and energy seemed condensed in the coarse cracks which made them look like a washerwoman's, though in fact she tended a small vegetable plot outside Freetown. Her purpose in life, unaided by an acute intelligence, was to give service to others. She wore a loose frock of bright print material and carpet slippers.

The two remaining women of the quartet were gaily attired in lappas and blouses and, being inarticulate, served as uncomprehending banner-wavers to the cause.

Dr Kawa stretched himself out on his chair, tilting it on to the back legs with affected composure. When he judged that they had had enough brandy to loosen their tongues, he asked what he could do for them. An interval of silence followed while the banner-wavers shuffled in their seats and the other two women exhanged glances and agreed it was time to begin.

'It's what we can do for you,' Mrs Coker replied.

'An even pleasanter surprise,' he said.

'We have come to discuss your marriage,' Mrs Coker said in a commanding tone which did not offer alternatives. The front legs of Dr Kawa's chair hit the floor with a crash.

'Indeed?' he said slowly, not knowing what line to take.

'Indeed!' she repeated.

He felt annoyed with himself for not having guessed

what they were up to. *What impertinence! To walk into my private life out of the blue and ask me to co-operate. But I must be tactful.* Pulling his chin thoughtfully, he was aware of a flicker of curiosity within himself about the full extent of the plot.

Mrs Coker, who did not like his silence, spoke next.

'It is a serious matter, Doctor. Grown-up women like us would not come all this way for nothing.'

Miss Baker felt that Mrs Coker had gone too far and tried to soften the effect with her kind appealing voice.

'Well, Doctor, a man like you; I mean! In your position you must have a woman. Grannie May does her best but she is old. You need a wife to brighten up the place with . . . with children. You know how our people are sensitive. They believe in family life and look up to a man who can take care of a family. It is for your own sake too.' Casting a sentimental glance round the walls she sighed with nostalgia spreading her lips in an expression of distress and pity. 'Not a single picture of your family on the wall. Ah! how well I remember your Grandpa . . . strong . . . and handsome . . .' she observed. But Mrs Coker, who had stiffened further with rage and disapproval at this unauthorized change in tactics, did not allow her to finish her reminiscence.

'Don't talk rubbish! The trouble with black women is that they are too sentimental,' she said lifting her nose higher. The admonished Miss Baker, somewhat upset, retired temporarily in silence, leaving Mrs Coker to conduct the negotiations. But the despotism in Mrs Coker's character did not stop at merely silencing Miss Baker.

'Besides, you know that since your accident you have not been able to think straight,' she added.

'Now Doctor,' she said turning to Dr Kawa and gathering her energies. 'Let's get to the point.' Her shoulder tips lifted slightly and her back arched faintly as if she was going to throw an asthmatic fit. She raised a warning index finger and her gaze met Dr Kawa's eyes. Her Victorian demeanour had given way to the fiery ghosts of her Fanti origin.

'The point is; if you will excuse me.' Her heavy breathing and the afterthought of her courtesy amused Dr Kawa and with difficulty he suppressed the laugh which swelled in his throat.

'The point is that it is unnatural for a man to be without a woman; and before you can be a leader of your people you must have a stable family life.' She paused for breath and then continued. 'Mind you, I know what goes on in other parts of the world – the so-called civilized countries, I'm sorry to say. But what do you expect if they don't know whether they're coming or going. And those women!' She paused again, almost overcome with emotion and acknowledged the approving sighs from the others.

'It makes my blood boil to think of it. Trying to be like men!' she gasped and turned her face away protectively from the vision which was bearing down on her and stimulating her resentment almost to a point beyond her powers of self-control.

Her anger was vented against the bosomless, unmenstruating women of Europe where sex was either absent or inter-substituted.

Yet the flame which singed her heart was fanned by the very air she breathed, and it was the excesses to which her daughters and granddaughters had abandoned themselves in their frenzy for progress which gnawed her soul. She remembered with bitterness that the last time the African lost his head he awoke to find himself enslaved. Here were her own women who had just discovered with early morning eagerness that they had legs and breasts – even brains. In the avalanche of their emancipation they had become aware of their sex organs – Eden all over again – every bit shining black. But what did she care if the sexes decided to compress themselves into one final outrageous orgasm?

The collective consciousness spoke through Mrs Coker's heightened vision as if she were in a trance. She could hear shouts through the window. Argument and counter argument.

You with the pointing finger, if you don't look out you'll find you've changed your sex and there's nothing you can do about it – it's nature. You've either got to go forwards or backwards– and now we've got so far and so clever, there's nothing for it but to go back and join the animals where we left them – free as air. You've got to realize that life walks within fixed limits – like a caged animal – like the food we eat – in at one end, round and round the middle, and out. What are you complaining about?

Just think: you want to be like animals. You want to return to the jungle. But it isn't there any more. Your jungle's wiped out – only swamps and desert. We are the survivors.

Bah! We'll make one. You watch. In less than fifty years we'll have a brand new shining jungle all over where the ice moved in and froze it the other day. This is the scientific age, remember. We can do anything we damn well please.

But the animals; what makes them noble is discipline. You can't get away from the word which you think disgusting. Plenty of instinct and discipline; that's what does it.

Discipline's for the man in the moon – he can have it. We're going free as air. What's the matter with you anyway? Are you living in the present or a couple of light years ago? Where did you get all those Greek ideas?

Mrs Coker saw in a consuming moment of awareness

the flash-back of centuries of the world's metamorphosis as if it were an X-ray film. But though she held the negative before her she could not translate the tortures into rational thought. She saw the chaos and was determined to overcome it. Against a background of prejudice and narrow-mindedness, conceit and ignorance, she would try to grasp the lilting raft which every moment seemed to be drifting out of reach.

When she spoke to Dr Kawa again, her voice was softer and sincere.

'There is your duty to the community, Doctor,' she said simply.

'We all have a duty, Mrs Coker – even that of broadening our minds,' he said, before he could stop himself. Mrs Coker felt the sting in his rejoinder but ignored it, remembering her own youth and the firm decision of a similar nature which she had once been called upon to make. She sighed heavily and her mask fell off her face and splintered on the floor. Her eyes took on a youthful charm and she showed the relaxed radiance of one who need no longer hide the truth.

'Well, Doctor, we have done what we can. The rest is up to you and your mother,' she said, and got up to leave.

Dr Kawa watched them go up the drive and out of sight before he shut the door. How many more such visits was he to expect?

He tried to settle the question with a large whisky.

Chapter Four

Dr Kawa rolled over in bed and embraced the woman he had been dreaming lay beside him. He woke, disturbed, because, though her body was well defined, her face was masklike, unrecognizable. The physiognomy was grotesque as if mutilated, though the expression was gentle. He rubbed his eyes and stretched his muscles. A shaft of light had forced its way through the window and lay beside him. Dr Kawa patted the bed affectionately.

Since the visit of the four women he had given serious thought to his future. He had decided that he needed a woman to companion him through life; his was not a celibate nature. But as yet he was unable to face the pallid prospect of marriage. What he needed most was an aesthetic love affair. One that was not rooted in the flesh alone. He must fall utterly and tragically in love – take the plunge. Yet he realized it was easier said than done. His had always been a protected life, burdened by compromises. He had never known what it was to endanger his security. It was difficult to change. Again one could not achieve such a love by design; it came from outside – the best he could do was to be prepared.

It was Sunday and he was alone with his thoughts. He leapt out of bed and pulled the curtains, letting the chatter of birds in the hibiscus blow in like incense. Next door he could hear them playing tennis. He made his bed with care and precision, tucking in the bottom of the sheet neatly and letting a flap hang free as he had seen the nurses do.

He went into the sitting-room and turned on the wireless. The waltzing voice of Mr Sylvester was apologizing to all his listeners for not having played all their requests. He found some coffee made in the kitchen and put it on to heat. He argued with himself whether to have a European or African breakfast, felt too lazy to do either and settled for coffee.

Outside, the perfect weather hung with the poise of a flower whose life seems foreshortened by the miracle of its beauty. The traffic was building up on the main accident-prone route to the sea and mile after chalky mile of beach. The earliest fugitives were European families with tents and dinghies on trailers. Behind them, prolific Lebanese families stacked high in large American cars rushed by in peristaltic waves. Some cars were the newest Cadillacs, others not so new with their exhaust pipes hanging loose and scraping the melting tar all the way. Some whizzed along with peppered haste; others with less respect for the comfort of their neighbours gave their children the horn to play with. The rear of the queue was brought up by scores of progressive Africans flying westward, grinding their wheels over their sorrows to overtake the others. All making hot haste to the sea and fresh air. All piling up their heart beats only to drown them under the rush of waves. Everybody was hurrying somewhere – to the roasting whiteness of the beaches, to dig little graves in the sand where they lay and waited for the sea to well up over them, hoping to be clean when they fitted their bones together again. Some went to sit under the palm trees with radio, bottle and thighs and rediscovered the lives they had left behind in the city. The beach was the line of conflict and absolution; the sea rushing in and the people crowding towards it with their cries.

They drove like demons and they drove blindfold just to take a sniff at the fresh air. Cyanosed and jaundiced multitudes, invalids hoping to be cured by a few cubic feet of ozone.

Where are you going?
To get away from it all.
What all?
We don't know and we're too tired to think. We have to get there before it's too late.

You've heard the rumour then, have you, that it's healthy to get out at week-ends? Now you're all going.

Do you ever see a white man's cemetery in Africa? It is not because they burn their corpses; they just don't die in Africa; not any more. They gave that up a long time ago; and don't blame the mosquito. If you want to know why, it's because they go to the seaside at week-ends and refresh themelves. And why should we leave it all to them? They're our beaches, aren't they?

But they have always been there – the beaches – and all you did was choke them with faeces.

What's that got to do with it? Are you a negrophobe, traitor? A negro yourself!

All I'm saying is that it's time you showed some sweat under your collar on your own account.

You keep sweating – we're off anyway. This is our country and we've been slaves long enough. Today the sun is shining and we're going to beat the white man at his own game with twice the zeul.

How about some hard work first, though?

Man, you judge a wedding by the bachelors' eve. Did you ever hear of a good wedding that did not start with a celebration?

41

Less celebration and more cerebration is what you need, if you ask me.

Well, we're not asking. They had more civilization for two thousand years and made a fine mess of it – why shouldn't we have the same right?

All right – if it's the right to destroy yourselves you're asking for here's a sharp axe – hack your children to pieces. Here's an automatic pistol – the best on the market. Blow your brains out and I'll watch.

Say, what are you anyway? What are you getting upset about? Are you a white man or a black Imperialist?

No, I'm burnt sugar black and had no choice in the matter. So I can ask questions and make a nuisance of myself until you throw off that hangover of self-pity and start doing something for yourselves.

That don't mean you can push me around and stop me getting rich and living proper.

I'd like to see you happy and not scared. I'd like to see black men happy because they've got more than the candle inside a magic lantern to be proud of. I want to see all men happy because it's the only way I can be happy. I want to see everything that lives drink in the sunlight and feel safe and warm inside.

*　　　*　　　*　　　*

The cars sweated in the blue heat and after them the coaches, church-loads of them, the motorcycles and the hikers. Horns hooting, engines belching, they flowed through the break in the dam which had held them back. They tore the air with the confusion of an air raid, because it was the philosophy of the day to flee.

*　　　*　　　*　　　*

The impatient hooting from a car which sounded as if it was in the drive brought him to his feet and to the window. A tall man in his thirties, handsome, moustached, stood by an Austin with the door open at the entrance to the drive next door. He was pressing the horn repeatedly, agitatedly. Presently a girl of about eight ran out of the house, stopped suddenly on the gravel path between the flower beds and stared at the young man with the car. Dr Kawa noticed the little girl's frilled white skirt and the red bow in her hair. The young man deigned to smile at her.

'Go away. Mama isn't coming. I hate . . . I hate you!' she shouted at the top of her voice and burst into tears. She threw herself among the flowers hiding her face, and shook with sobs.

The smart young man, taking no notice of the child, continued to honk his horn with even greater vigour, then with a sweeping gesture of disgust sat himself in the car. Soon a pretty, fair-skinned woman came running out of the house, across the gravel towards the sulking cupid in the car. She had thick black eyebrows and full breasts. She had barely got in beside him when he backed the car and joined the stampede on the road.

The child stopped crying as soon as the car had gone and sat dreamlike among the flowers. Her eyes glittered with the solemn anger known only to children. She got up and walked slowly round the far side of the house twisting her index finger in the folds of her skirt. The people on the tennis court were too busy to notice her. Dr Kawa returned to his chair and a book.

A few moments later he heard hurrying footsteps outside and waited for the knock before he opened the door.

'Dr Kawa? My name is Marshall. I live next door. Sorry to trouble you like this,' said the man at the door somewhat breathlessly. Dr Kawa invited his visitor in and showed him to a chair. Both men sat in silence for a moment observing each other.

Marshall was well covered but not obese. His complexion was a cross between a negro and a Lebanese. You would not have judged him sensitive from his appearance, yet there was something timid and gentle about him which was endearing. Dr Kawa noted the head sloping away from a prominent forehead along a central baldness flanked by an arc of greying hair. The eyes were perfectly ordinary and straightforward, yet easy to remember. Mr Marshall seemed self-conscious about his rather large sloping nose. Although his chest was covered in coils of black hair he did not give the impression of physical strength, rather he had the quality of survival and obstinate moral endurance. He was a type who, to everyone's astonishment, became a hero in adversity; at least that was Dr Kawa's first estimation of him.

Mr Marshall's obsession with his nose led him to be constantly rubbing, twisting or keeping it out of sight with his hands, and this habit made his voice sound muffled. He spoke grammatically correct English with a Freetown accent; a series of musical onomatopaeic ejaculations interspersed with words.

Dr Kawa had heard of Mr Marshall that his house was worth seeing, his wife worth having and his nobility of soul worth despising.

Mr Marshall on the other hand thought Dr Kawa looked young for his age, sensitive to the point of romanticism, but concealed this with a tendency to aloofness and a beard. His eyes were brooding, his mouth determined, reliable as a colleague and faithful as a friend. He thought he would like Dr Kawa.

'Have a drink, won't you?' Dr Kawa began.

'Yes. Brandy, please.' Dr Kawa filled two glasses and sat down.

'Sorry, this is an awkward time to call, I know. I had . . . I mean we had meant to ask you over for dinner but . . . but . . .' He broke off, as if looking for a plausible excuse. 'But there's plenty of time. You won't be going up country yet,' he said finally.

'I have been admiring your house and envying you,' Dr Kawa said.

'Yes it is nice. But houses are like coconuts. You never know if they are rotten until you see the inside. You must come and play tennis. We have a club, you know.'

'Yes, I hear you playing sometimes. I'd love to come and have a game.'

'Well, how's the practice, Doc?' Mr Marshall broke out, as if desiring to create an intimate atmosphere.

'Not bad; picking up.'

'I could get you a lot more patients, Lebanese patients. They have the money, you know.'

'Thank you very much, but I'm doing enough for any one man at the moment,' Dr Kawa said, chuckling to himself.

'I believe in people helping each other, Doc.'

'So do I. Especially neighbours.'

'Exactly. Look, you mustn't keep to yourself. Come round and see us. Come and have fun,' Mr Marshall said.

'As soon as work gets a little lighter you will have to keep me off your tennis court by force,' Dr Kawa said.

'This is just a social call, you understand, but I would like you to be my doctor. I have heard good things about you and I'd like to be one of your private patients.'

'Oh yes, but who's your doctor at the moment?'

'Never mind that, Doc. The thing is that I don't trust him.'

'I'm sure you'll agree that it's a delicate matter and I can't just steal my colleagues' patients like that.'

'But it is my money. Good money too, Doc. Can't I have whom I like?'

'No doubt you can. But —' Dr Kawa began.

'Well I'll tell you. What the hell. All he cares about is my money. He doesn't care a damn about me. I know. I'm no fool, Doc. I can tell from the look in his eyes and the way he holds the syringe when he gives me an injection. Inside he's laughing at me all the time; like everybody else. They say my wife has cut off my balls.'

Dr Kawa cleared his throat and said nothing.

'Besides you are my neighbour – that means something more to a man.'

'Please don't misunderstand me. I have no reason for not wanting to take you over as a patient but it's unethical and . . .'

'Ethics be damned, man! You always hear these words – words! Just words! but you never find anyone who can show you what it is – in tangible terms. It doesn't mean a damn thing – not a damn thing.' He was breathing more quickly.

'How is it, Doc, that with all the science, all the wonderful discoveries, nobody can help a pain inside the heart? a pain that is there when you go to sleep and is still there when you wake? You have to put up with it – that's what they spit in your face. Is that what you tell your patients, Doc? Nothing I can do – you have to put up with it. Is it?'

'There are times when however nicely you try to word the phrase it only comes to the same thing,' Dr Kawa said.

'But you do try, Doc. You try to soften it.'

'Most people do, I think,' Dr Kawa replied.

46

'No! Most people say: You've got to put up with it. If you'd had the sense to cut your heart out and hang it up to dry like the rest of us, you wouldn't have had that pain. It's your own damned fault. That's what they say.'

'I don't see what you're driving at,' Dr Kawa said in his best consulting-room style. Not overprompting, not leading, but encouraging the patient to tell his own story.

'Never mind anyway,' Mr Marshall replied sharply; then with sudden feeling, 'Look Doc, you must come and see us. My wife and I need friends, true friends.'

'Yes, I had meant to call on you but . . .' Dr Kawa began.

'You have heard, of course,' Mr Marshall interrupted. 'Heard?'

'Heard about me and my wife. That there is an awkwardness. I'm surprised if you haven't because everybody knows about it. But the people who sympathize with you are the ones who laugh behind your back because they don't give a twopenny damn and you know why? Because they are rotten inside themselves. So rotten that they themselves can't bear the smell. So what do they do? They lose their sense of smell so they can't smell at· all.' He paused and his breathing became heavy and irregular. The bottle tinkled and the glasses were filled.

'As a matter of fact, she's just gone out with her boy friend,' Mr Marshall resumed.

'I'm very sorry,' Dr Kawa said.

'But what can I do? I love the woman. We can't just stop loving because there is difficulty, war or famine. Can we? But look, Doc. I have the feeling that we are going to see more of each other. Clara would like to meet you, and she always gets her own way. She's that kind of woman.'

'Of course I'd like to get to know you both. I am naturally very sorry about the circumstances.'

'Actually that is one reason why I came. I wanted to talk to somebody; to get it off my chest, as it were. Also I wanted to tell you about Clara and about us before rumours turn you against her. You see it is difficult for me to say this, but I have failed. I have not been able to give her what she is looking for, and yet I know in my blood that she needs love and friendship, and despite everything I try to give her what I can. Do you understand, Doc?'

'I think so.'

Mr Marshall's voice became distant and unreal like a voice in a dream. He drained his glass noisily before he began his story . . .

'Ten years ago I was forty-two. My business was doing well and I was contented. I was up country at Moyamba at the time. It was the height of the rainy season and you know what this is like. As luck would have it I went down with some gut infection which the doctor called Gastro-erti . . .'

'Gastro-enteritis,' Dr. Kawa prompted.

'That's it; and I was in bed . . . oh . . . oh! three weeks or so. Old mammy Banya who looked after the house unfortunately caught the germ, and, I'm sorry to say, died of it. She was a good woman. She had been with me a long time since the days when I was trying to make two ends meet! However, before she got ill she had arranged for her grandchild to take over in the house. She was a raw Mende girl; beautiful . . . you know, that sort of beauty you can't put your finger on. Quiet, fresh like a new moon. She did not speak a word of English or Krio; apparently her parents had died when she was a child and

48

there was no money to send her to school. This girl looked after me through that illness. Never saying very much; just smiling and nursing me.

'As I got better, I began to teach her a few words of English and each day I would give her an hour's lesson, which lengthened as my strength returned; and she learnt quickly. Well, one day she was sitting on the floor beside my bed as usual and repeating the sentences which I read from a book. Suddenly I realized she had not repeated the phrase I had just read. Surprised, I took off my spectacles and looked at her. Lord help me! Those black eyes with their heavy black eyebrows. I thought I was looking down a well and instinctively drew back to stop myself falling into it. I felt empty in my chest. Scooped out as those boys scoop the coconut out of its shell. I was in love with her, and believe me, there's nothing as poignant as love when it comes late in life. There I was stricken by love at forty-two on top of my Gastro-tri . . .'

'Gastro-enteritis.'

'Gastro-enteritis. Anyway, to cut a long story short, I married her.'

'Did she love you?' Dr Kawa asked.

'You know that tribal customs don't countenance love marriages in the ordinary sense, but that does not mean they are not capable of love. On the contrary, I am convinced that she loved me. At forty-two a man knows when a woman loves him and when she's only trying to.'

Dr Kawa's voice sounded more relaxed and a little involved when he spoke next.

'How old was she?'

'Eighteen. So you get the point. Lovely as she was, she was still unmarried. At the time I thought it was because the old grandmother had no money for her dowry but later I got to know the real reason – I shall tell you about that. At the time all my friends were against the marriage. They thought that I was a fool. She was too young. She'd never come up to scratch, they said. Some of them even broke off our friendship.'

'Did you think you were doing her a good turn? Were you sorry for her? Were you trying to prove something, perhaps?' Dr Kawa asked.

'Not a bit of it. No experiment; no pity. It was the first time in forty-two years that I discovered what it was like to love a woman. To want to make her a part of your life, even to die for her. In my younger days I had been too busy making money and looking for security to bother about love. Now I had money and love. We came down to town and I bought this plot of land next door and built that very house. There was nothing I could do to make her happy that I did not do. For me it was as if life had started all over again. You know what a little whitewash round an orange tree can do for it; it makes it blossom. That was just what she did for me. I began to see myself differently, and the world changed too. I felt I had begun to understand at last that love was understanding – ultimate awareness!

'We had not been in the house long when my young nephew came to "Adoo". He stayed with us, cleaned shoes in the morning, helped the servants – that sort of thing. His mother, my half-sister, had a lot to cope with. You see I am Lebanese on my mother's side; and she hoped I would do something for the boy. And I had plans for him. Oh yes! I had put him in a good school but he wasn't serious and was always out swimming during school hours. Somehow he didn't fall in with us as young people usually do. He seemed to have a grudge somewhere – I don't know.' Mr Marshall's voice was calm and objective like that of an uninvolved witness.

'Anyhow he got impatient. This was the time when our boys took it into their heads that London was paved with gold, and were risking life and limb to get there. Early one morning his mother came with tears in her eyes to say that Freddie had sent a message saying he was a stowaway on his way to London. That was that!

'We never heard from him again but my sister used to get news that he was having a pretty rough time. No gold, no money, no food; and the cold winters. I used to send him some money from time to time through his mother.

'Within three years you could not have guessed that Clara, that's my wife, had never spoken a word of English until I met her. She was radiant ... and ... she was a joy! I decided to send her to London for a brushing up. I could not leave the business for very long at the time, but I took her myself and got her a flat in Hampstead, and left her with friends who were only too pleased to help her. I came home. After nine months she returned home and brought my nephew back with her. It turned out they had been living together in London sharing the £100 a month I was allowing her. It has gone on ever since.' Mr Marshall paused and cleared his throat.

'Well, we had two children by then. Sonia who is now eight, and Clarissa. Until then I did not know that love's growth is boundless, and I was more than ever in love with Clara. Her beauty had that extra sparkle which sophistication gives a woman, like fresh fruit on a well-laid table. Moreover I was convinced that their affair was a passing phase that she had felt sorry for him, lonely and starving as he was in the London fog – but you know our saying that it is always the soft-hearted woman who gets a bastard! I pleaded with her to give him up. I was prepared to forget what had gone on in London. Now she was home we could start afresh. But it seems sophistication had hardened her. I went down on my knees; I begged her to think of our children. I promised to do anything; give her anything she wished. I know that was foolish but I was distraught. Do you know what she told me? You can't buy love with money. So I spent more money. I made the house even more comfortable and built a tennis court, but to no avail.

'Things went steadily from bad to worse. She was constantly out with him, and people began to talk. The children never saw her. The whole thing had become an open scandal. She made a fool of me all right.

'Things came to a head one Sunday morning. I had gone to Mass as usual. I had prayed and prayed for understanding between us, and when I left the church I was feeling much better. My daughter Sonia was six then and knew the sound of my car when the engine slowed down to turn into the drive. She rushed towards the gate crying, so that it was only by the grace of God that I did not run over her. I got out of the car and she fell on me burying her face in my legs; I tell you she was shaking like a leaf. I did not know a child could feel so deeply. Between her sobs she said that she had gone into her mother's bedroom and had found that man fighting with her in bed. She cried, "He tore off Mummy's clothes and Mummy had no clothes on. I *beat* him, Daddy. I did. I told him to get off Mummy. I never want to see him again. He's a bad man."'

'Good Heavens!' Dr Kawa muttered with suppressed agitation. 'Did you not think of a divorce?'

'We are Roman Catholics, you see. Anyway the love I have for her is not destructive. There isn't a single day during which I have not thought of killing them both, but I could never do it.' Mr Marshall spoke with the calm resolution of one who had temporarily transferred his sorrow on to someone else's shoulders.

'You value her above your happiness and honour?'

'My happiness is in her. As for honour – it is only a wind of passion like anger. I keep hoping that one day she will come back for good. If she came back today I would forgive her.'

'I don't know what to say,' confessed Dr Kawa.

'You know, when I get over my daily attacks of madness when I have wanted to crush the life out of her, I have asked myself what is life worth without love? And the answer has always been nothing! Nothing at all.'

'But if you can't get a divorce, couldn't you separate? Let him take her away? That would at least save your children to some extent.'

'He hasn't any money. He's got nothing. She'd go to . . . she'd become something awful if I let that happen.'

'So you let them carry on under your own roof.'

'But she doesn't love him. One can't love a vacuum.'

'But she has said quite plainly that she does not love you,' Dr Kawa said with growing exasperation.

'You see, I think like this. Love is like the stars. It gives – they shine, because it is their nature, even when the clouds come between them and us they are still shining up there.'

'She must have love for someone if not for you or your children.'

'She thinks she loves him but she can't because love is not destructive. If she loved him she would not go about it this way. That makes me sorry for her and it strengthens my love.

'One day when I am dead she will realize how much I loved her but then it will be too late. You know, Doc, we always wait till it's too late. I expect you see a lot of patients like that. Wait! wait! wait! Wait till the rain stops, wait till the sun shines; wait till I've had a good time; wait till there's some money in the bank; and then bang! It's too late.

'But my children worry me. I'm no philosopher, Doc. I can't think beyond my nose and my family, really; and God knows I have no ambitions of handing on the family flame and all that. But if I could give my children the chance of a fair start – if I could help them to find their own way in life – I owe it to them.' He hesitated as if to let the words sink in. 'To be responsible for the denial to one's children of a clean page in life is the most terrible unhappiness. One might just as well not have children. You didn't see Sonia's eyes that Sunday morning. They were fierce and full of hatred. I tell you they were looking into the grave, man! A girl of six. Do you think she's had a fair chance? Do you?'

'I don't know what to think. Somehow you have made me feel personally responsible as well,' Dr Kawa said.

'But I tell you; that Sunday morning when I got back from church,' Mr Marshall continued, his voice shaking with the strain of controlling his emotions, 'I was feeling calm inside. I thought God had entered into me; at the same time as Satan was entering my house. There I was with Sonia by the gate. I picked her up and kissed her, wiping her tears with my handkerchief. Then she told me what had happened. I put her down and held her hand because I was afraid of dropping her. She looked at me as if to say "Can't you do anything? Even you?" What could I say? How do you console or hoodwink a child who suddenly loses something more valuable than eyesight? A child who has been run over by the truth and stunned?

'I left the car blocking the gate and walked with Sonia to the house. By that time I did not know what I was doing. Slowly we climbed the stairs to the bedroom on the first floor. Sonia began to scream and struggle. She said she did not want to go into that room again. I held her firmly as we stood in front of the door. She continued to struggle. I kicked the door open. It was unlocked and the room was empty. The bed was unmade. I think perhaps I would have killed them then.

'I stepped into the room and Sonia held on to the banisters so as not to follow me. She was still screaming as if the place was haunted. Then I remember letting go of her hand. I heard a smooth gliding noise. When I pulled myself back to the landing Sonia was lying motionless at the foot of the stairs. The next few moments were . . . I don't remember quite what happened. I remember picking her up and holding her to my chest. I was convinced she was dead. I remember shouting, "She is dead; I have killed her", as I walked up and down the stairs with Sonia in my arms. Then the nice young man who lived here at the time – from Yorkshire – came in and took her away from me. I remember him saying, "Nonsense, she's nothing of the sort", and I passed out.

'When I woke up it was dark and my sister was sitting by my bed. She told me the child was all right and would only be in hospital a few days.

'I told her I had to go to Freetown. She said there was no need; that the child was all right and the doctor said I was to spend the evening in bed. I'm sorry to say I was a bit rough with her. I got up, put my dressing-gown over my pyjamas and asked her to drive me into town. She thought I was mad of course but she did as I wished. I was still dazed, as you can well imagine, and I don't remember very much about the drive into town. But the sound of water flowing under Jockey Bridge I do remember. What a waste of blood: all that blood flowing into the sea, I kept thinking. That was how it struck me. I also remember the crowds along Kroo Town Road, the cars hooting and the lights flashing; then down Westmoreland Street. At Cotton Tree my sister asked if I wanted to go straight to the hospital or to her place first. But I wasn't thinking of going to the hospital. I did not answer. She nudged me on the arm. "Jackie," she said, "We are almost there. Do you want to go to the hospital?" "Take me to the Bishop," I said.

'Well, my sister has had a hard life one way and another and she really isn't easily shocked or frightened, but she was that night. By God she was. If she had suspected that I was mad before, she was convinced of it by then, and that frightened her. When women stop arguing with you, then you know you're either mad or they've finished with you.

'Anyhow, she drove me to the Bishop's Residence down Wilberforce Street and waited in the car.' The brandy had made his delivery more light-hearted and he injected a note of comedy into his story.

'This was about nine o'clock at night. I rang the bell and waited. I rang a second time and then I heard a little window squeaking. You see, there's a little window just beside the door and the glass is painted in such a way that he can see you but you can't see him.

'I was feeling a little more myself by this time and conscious of my dress. The wind was blowing furiously and storm clouds hung over the hills. Perhaps it was the dressing-gown more than anything which made him open the door. I don't know. Anyway he opened the door in astonishment with a glass of port in one hand.

'"Come in; come in, my son," he said, shutting the

56

door behind me. You know how priests like to think themselves virile – pity they are never put to the test,' Mr Marshall chuckled with a noise like falling rock. 'But I was not in a humorous mood then, I can tell you. He led me half-way down the passage and turned round to me. "What in heaven's name is the matter?", he said, but as I did not want to talk in the passage I did not answer. He showed me into the study. "Sit down: sit down. In all the twenty years that I've been a priest I've never seen anything quite so dejected-looking as you," he said. "That wife of yours again?"

'"More than that, Father; it's my daughter this time." So I told him the story from start to finish.

'"Your wife is a humbug I'm bound to admit, but I have told you a dozen times what the Church's teaching on divorce is. Rome does not permit it. Marriage is a solemn and indissoluble union."

'"I know that, Father, but what can I do? If I had a pain in my kidneys I would go to a doctor. Now I have an ache in my soul, I have come to you."

'"But how can I help? We must learn to bear the Cross of Calvary."

'"It appears that the weight is not equally shared," I said.

'"That is not for you to decide, my son. Your share of the burden of this life is only a minor complement to salvation in the next."

'"But tell me Father, is the doctrine of the Church more important than people and life itself? Where would the Church be without men and women?" I asked him.

'"We must not probe too far into these matters lest we become guilty of blasphemy. But I will say this. It is a common fallacy of our time for Man to think, and I use the word in the generic sense, that all creation revolves round him. And by a lapse in his spiritual logic, he forgets that we are only God's creatures. If you are asking me whether life and love can be equated with advantage against the Doctrine of the Temporal Church – then my answer is that we are skating on thin ice here. But if on the other hand the equation is as against the Church Eternal, then as good soldiers of the Cross, the Church's doctrine must come first."

'"But what about my children, Father? Destroyed at so early an age. Is not this life a preparation for the next? Cannot the Church on earth allow them a fair start?"

'"It is stated in the Commandments that He will visit the sins of the fathers upon the third and fourth generation."

'"In other words, one rotten banana ruins the lot!" I said.

'"And will show mercy to thousands who love Him and keep His Commandments," he said.

'"If only I could see where the chain breaks, Father. Where redemption comes in," I pleaded.

'"You have your confessional. You can seek forgiveness there."

'"That is the point. I have done nothing wrong. I cannot confess for my wife; nevertheless, I am rooted in sin through the indissolubility of our marriage. How can I prevent her sins rubbing off on to my children without the Church's help? After all, you married us."

'"You can pray for her and them. But we must also beware of judging ourselves and others," he said.

'By this time I was more depressed and confused than ever.'

'He practically told you to go home and bear your cross,' Dr Kawa said.

'That's right,' Mr Marshall agreed.

'The hoarse voice of centuries of worn-out religion,' Dr Kawa added.

'The long and short of it was that he tapped me on the shoulder, gave me his blesssing and showed me the door. When I got home the house was empty. My younger daughter Clarissa was away with her grandmother. I don't know if you have ever experienced extreme loneliness. I was afraid to go inside the house. It was like a tomb. How does one express it? It was an oppressive loneliness . . . as . . . as if I alone inhabited the universe. Could it have been the same feeling that made Sonia refuse to go into the bedroom that morning? I stood there by the door and watched the black clouds heavy with rain. A flash of lightning brightened the sky from end to end, and the rain began to carpet the ground.

'I dropped my dressing-gown and pyjamas on the steps and fell under the sharp drops of rain. They really felt like nails piercing my skin. I rubbed myself with the gravel and let the water pour over me. The effect was amazing. After half an hour I felt as if I had been thrashed with thorns and that my entire body was bleeding; but inside I was calm again. As calm as after confession. I went to bed and fell instantly asleep. My wife walked in three days later as if nothing had happened.'

'What about Sonia? Was she all right?' asked Dr Kawa.

'Thank God she was. There was no fracture or anything serious. But when she came home she was changed. The doctor said it was the late effect of shock. She . . . she behaved as if she had got a lot older. Not the same child at all. She was quiet and reserved : too much so for a girl of her age. Tell me, Doc. This is something that really worries me. Do children commit suicide?'

'I don't know. I don't know the answer to that one.

I've never seen or heard of it at that age,' Dr Kawa said.

'It sticks in my chest like a bad cold. Right in here. Every time I call her and she doesn't answer I think she's done it! That fear can drive a man crazy.'

'Has she shown any signs of being unstable?'

'Nothing more than I've told you. She's quiet and too reserved. But it's when I look at her eyes that I worry. There's something in them that wasn't there before.' He sighed and paused for a long time as if in thought.

'Well, it's lunch time. I'm sorry I've bothered you. Thanks for listening, and do come over and see us any time at all.'

'Certainly I will,' Dr Kawa said.

The two men walked out into the bare heat of the afternoon sun and Mr Marshall disappeared through a weakness in the hedge and waved as he walked towards the house.

Chapter Five

Sports Day was the most important event of the year at Aggrey School. At its approach, mathematics and Religious Knowledge retired to their summer hibernation for at least four weeks. But its effect on the pupils varied. For the 'book boys' it was an unhappy time. They were ruthlessly persecuted for all the prizes they could not help winning during the previous year, while for the athletic types it was worth all the red marks across their copy books.

Jonah was an instinctive 'book boy'. He was thin, timid, inclined to be sickly, and a prefect. It was his duty as prefect to present each morning to the Principal a list of all boys who had been late for prayers and those who had come to school bare-foot. Shoes had become compulsory and therefore revolted against by many of the boys. Jonah knew that the boys carried their shoes in their satchels until they were in sight of the gates before they put them on, but he was not sympathetic to the rule and preferred not to see the loopholes. These were the civlizing days when shoes had replaced books in importance.

On a Friday morning Jonah was summoned to the Principal's office. As he climbed the ink-stained stairs he had grave misgivings because he knew the Principal was the sort of man described as long-suffering; this meant that instead of having a boy flexed edgewise over a table and giving him a dozen strokes, he vented his displeasure by the liberal dispensing of 'moral tonics'. These either took the form of the boy finding himself at the bottom of his form for the term, or of his father receiving a stern reminder that his boy could not expect a helpful testimonial by which to procure his future advancement, when it would be the school's pleasure to shed him on the world at large. Jonah had recently found himself in the Principal's bad books.

Jonah knocked feebly at the door of the Principal's office and waited. No answer came; not even the shuffling of papers from inside, but he knew that no one ever entered the office without knocking at least twice, so he knocked again, more firmly.

'Come in!' came the faint and distant response of a man much harassed by work. Jonah opened the door, stepped inside and hesitated, to allow the Principal to change his mind.

'Come in and close the door. Keep the draught out,' the Principal said.

Jonah moved nimbly into the office shutting the door behind him, his knees shaking involuntarily. The Principal sat at his desk frowning at some papers, and did not look up. His upper lip was screwed up characteristically as if the room was full of bad smells. Jonah moved forward and stood with his hands behind his back expecting the worst. His heart fluttered almost to a standstill.

'What is it?' the Principal asked at length, pretending absent-mindedness.

'You sent for me, sir?'

He looked at Jonah over his half-lenses with the persistence of a judge who does not believe the evidence and trusts his own dissecting powers to shell out the truth.

'Ah! yes,' he said, resting his papers and leaning back in his rotating chair, his large hands cradled over his stomach. He stared at Jonah for some time, then appeared to have come to a decision.

'You know I have a good mind to punish you?'

'You have a perfect right, sir,' Jonah replied before he could stop himself. The Principal's eyes tightened.

'You were very rude to me the other afternoon.'

'Rude, sir?'

'Yes, rude. You've got a good brain, Jonah, but you won't use it. All these novels you read instead of doing your work won't get you anywhere. Luckily for you I know your mother well. We went to school together, that's why I have been so patient with you.'

Jonah tried to say thank you but could not form the words. Instead he murmured something about the heat.

'This is not the first hot weather we've had in Africa. Anyway, that wasn't why I sent for you.'

Jonah's knees buckled with relief as if they had been struck from behind, and he held on momentarily to the desk.

'Dr Kawa is coming to give the boys a Medical before Sports Day. I want you to look after it.'

'Pardon, sir?'

'Don't you ever listen to what's being said, boy?'

'Oh yes, the Medical, sir. When, sir?'

'One day next week . . . where's my diary?' He searched through piles of loose sheets of paper on his desk, found his diary and stretched out his neck like a turtle to read.

'Mon-d-day, the 24th,' he said, putting it away.

'What am I to do, sir?'

'How long have you been in the school, Jonah?'

'Five years, sir.'

'And how long have you been a prefect?'

63

'Nearly two, sir.'

'And you don't know what to do for a Medical Examination?'

'I have never conducted one, sir. The head prefect always does that himself.'

'He is away for a week. That is why you have to do it.'

'Yes, sir.'

'Use the sixth-form room for the examinations – it's larger – and the fifth for changing in. There will be no sports practice on that day. Remind me to announce it during Assembly. Can't have them breathless and reeking of sweat during their Medical,' he added, picking up his papers.

'May I ask another question, sir?'

'If it isn't impertinent.'

'What was the doctor's name, sir?'

'Kawa. K-A-W-A. An Old Boy of whom we are very proud.' With that he dismissed Jonah.

*   *   *   *

The day of the examinations was overcast and miserable, made even worse by a biting wind. Nature herself seemed to be in the agonizing throes of parturition out of which she would bless the earth with the ecstasy of stillness and rebirth. In the classroom the doors and windows remained closed and the lights were turned on. The boys chattered restlessly and noisily, moved by a warm animalism in anticipation of a storm. But the clouds held on to their moisture and not a flash of lightning seared the thick mists which flowed lazily down the valleys in the distance. The dark clouds looked infinitely more powerful than the soft skies of smiling days or even the self-indulgent raging of midsummer suns. The burnt clumps of grass on the rock faces of the hills merged imperceptibly into the moss-green darkness of the cloud shadows.

Jonah was alone in the sixth-form room which, except for a chair, table and wash-basin, had been stripped of its furniture for the purposes of the examination. As the minutes passed he became increasingly nervous in case he should have forgotten some important detail. From time to time he rushed to the window which looked out over the drive. Jonah was aware of a state of mind that was new to him. He realized that he actually wanted to give a good account of himself and of the school. The unexpected projection of this new image of himself increased his agitation. To him it was a different aspect of himself, but really it was only his first awareness of it. Chin in hand, he wandered round the room. 'What have I forgotten?' he mused. A couch. He would most likely need a couch. Where can I find a couch?' He observed the clock on the wall. It seemed silent and impassive as if it bore no relation to lifetime. At any one moment its arms were static whereas inside he was rolling over with enthusiasm. 'He is due any time! No hope of producing a couch now! Why hadn't I thought of it before? Would it be any use arranging two tables end on? No; it would be unkind to the boys.'

When Dr Kawa arrived Jonah was by his car to meet him.

'Dr Kawa, sir? I am Jonah, one of the prefects. We are ready for you upstairs,' he began. It was drizzling and Dr Kawa offered a wet hand. Jonah's eyes were dull and moist as usual, as if he had just been in a driving wind, and contrasted with the dark, almost glittering eyes of Dr Kawa who took his bag from the back seat and they walked with Jonah towards the cloisters and the steps.

'I don't suppose you will find much has changed since you were here, sir,' Jonah said, to break the silence. Dr

Kawa contemplated the ink-stains on the wooden steps with nostalgia.

'No, perhaps it's just as well. But I don't remember having these Medicals before Sports Day when I was here. I think it was assumed that we were all healthy in those days, and those who weren't were lazy.'

Jonah said he didn't think the attitude had changed much.

They reached the Principal's office and Jonah was about to knock when Dr Kawa held his arm.

'By the way, I shall put myself entirely in your hands. You introduce me to the routine,' he said.

Jonah nodded and knocked.

'Come in,' came the distant and martyred voice of the Principal. He knocked again, opened the door and announced Dr Kawa. Mr Hamilton sprang from his chair as if he had been caught asleep and came towards them warmly with quick anthropoid steps. He and Dr Kawa met and clasped hands like long separated friends.

'My dear boy,' Mr Hamilton said, lost for words. Jonah had never seen him like this. He seemed suddenly to have shed his cloak of age and was radiant with vitality. His pendant lower lip was rescued in a smile and his brown eyes moistened. He seemed unable to speak for an embarrassing moment while he held the other's hand in his and looked him over as a craftsman would examine a piece of work well done, or a father a repentant prodigal. When he spoke again his voice was a whine of affection.

'I can hardly believe my eyes,' he said with more gentle scrutiny.

'It's very nice to see you again. I must confess that I had not expected to find you here – it's an added pleasure,' Dr Kawa said.

66

'Confess, my boy, that's what we're here for, said Mr. Hamilton, partly regaining his headmasterly omnipotence. 'Thought I would have been thrown out, eh?' Mr Hamilton had never enjoyed discussing his retirement and seemed momentarily upset.

'Thought I would have been thrown out, eh?' he repeated, as he showed Dr Kawa to a chair opposite his own.

Dr Kawa said, 'It's remarkable, really! Thought you would have had enough of the new generation.'

Mr Hamilton was one of those men who continue to be indispensable even when they appear redundant, like a favourite mistress. For several years his retirement had been insisted on by the young men of the domestic Press, who were so busy producing a revolution that they had not considered the situation to follow. Those were bridges to be crossed when they got to them. What if there were no bridges? They hadn't thought of that; and while they ranted and piled abuse on the soft-livered men of the old generation, Mr Hamilton had gone on steadily with his work like the old Cotton Tree which was both the physical and psychological centre of Freetown, gently dropping his leaves.

The Principal's office was a defaced model of Victoriana; floor boards withering with too zealous scrubbing, dusty red velvet curtains which slid along brass rings on rods, and walls stacked with books and papers labelled *Educational Edicts*. One section of the room was curtained off and screened a primus stove.

Mr Hamilton assumed his attitude of speech-making from his chair.

'Well, Dr Kawa, we have watched your career with interest, and I for one am very proud of your achievements, and so is the school.'

'Thank you.'

'A first-class degree from Cambridge and a Gold Medal in Obstetrics mean a lot out here. I know people don't really understand the intrinsic value . . . to them the words conjure up glamour . . . but, no, it indicates a *mens sana*. Yes, a *mens sana*. It is the spirit behind it.'

'I find values rather difficult to determine at present.'

'You're not alone.' Mr Hamilton looked in Jonah's direction.

'Well, do you find it strange coming home to the Dark Continent?'

'The first impact is naturally overwhelming; one gets out of the habit of mirth and vitality.'

Mr Hamilton nodded. 'I remember when I came back from the States some thirty years ago. This school was no more than a few huts linked by a large number of snakes.'

'The snakes hadn't quite gone when I was here.'

'Well, they were about one per cent of what we found in the early days. Well, here I was, stuck in my own country with a Government which looked down on my American degree. There was nothing to do; nothing except roll up my sleeves and grab a tool. I haven't looked back since.' He paused and gentleness filled his face. 'So you see; when I look at you like this – destined for success, all my sleepless nights and even my stomach ulcer seem worthwhile.' His face expanded with delight. 'It is a great moment in my life; enough to make me weep tears of joy.' Mr Hamilton's cheeks vibrated under a smile, and for a moment Jonah thought real tears would roll down his face. He clenched his fists with embarrassment and disappeared behind the curtain to make some coffee. His precautions were unnecessary.

'Such a problem, resolving one's duty to the community and one's individual needs; not easy,' Dr Kawa said thoughtfully.

'Too true. Too true. I may say that when rumours were circulating to the effect that you were going to make your home in England, I felt your problem, and was able to discount the rumours. Some of us are made pioneers against our wishes and there's no shirking it. You had to come home to find your place of rest, and it was only a question of time before your conscience would rebel against exile. After all, who will build Africa if we don't?'

Jonah poured out some coffee and handed it round. Mr Hamilton produced a bottle of brandy from his drawer.

'Do you indulge?' he asked, uncapping the bottle.

'It's just the sort of weather for it, but I won't, thank you.'

'Well I do for my rheumatism. I know you doctors don't subscribe to the theory that it does keep the cold out of the joints, but then you can't know everything.' He searched for and found a small medicine glass into which he dispensed a measure of brandy against the light, poured it into his coffee and drank the lot in one gulp, after very careful stirring.

'That's better. That's much better.'

When Dr Kawa had finished his coffee, Mr Hamilton got up.

'Well I mustn't keep you. Jonah will look after you and if there's anything you need, just let me know.' He walked to the door with them. As he shook hands he said to Dr Kawa, 'Will you have lunch with me here at say, 12.45? I've asked some of the senior members of staff to come and meet you.'

'Great chap,' Dr Kawa said as they walked along the windy veranda to begin the Medical.

'Rather fond of giving advice, though.'

'Talks more sense than many men of his age. I'm afraid we led him quite a dance in the old days. Of course, he wasn't Principal then, and he didn't seem to mind the pranks!'

'We like him too, but he is getting old and tired and does not enjoy practical jokes any more. In fact, he's gone a bit sour,' Jonah said.

They entered the empty classroom and Jonah apologized for not having a couch. Dr Kawa said he didn't need one, and that if he did have one it would take twice as long to get through the work. Jonah felt completely at ease and liked him.

Dr Kawa opened his leather case on the table, and took out a stethoscope, a torch and several shining instruments from a black box lined with blue velvet where they had been nicely packed like chocolates. He sat down and looked through a pile of printed sheets which were on the table in front of him. Each had a name, age and address column and down the left side a tabulated description of various parts of the body.

'This is my guide, is it? Well, shall we begin?'

Jonah rang a little bell and his first victim came running, stripped to the waist.

'Saidu Kamara?'

'Yes, sir.'

'How old are you?'

'Fourteen, sir.'

He ticked it off on the sheet.

'What form are you in now?'

'Junior Cambridge form next year, sir.'

'Have you had any illnesses, Kamara?'

'No sir, nothing serious.'

'Good. Anything at all, any minor illnesses?'

'No sir,' without hesitation. He was ticked off on the sheet.

'Has anyone in your family had any illnesses?'

'No sir, but we all have worms, sir.'

'How long have you had them?'

'Always, sir. We have castor oil and worm medicine every Saturday, sir.' Saidu screwed up his face and seemed to shudder at the thought.

'How do you know you've got them?'

'I've seen them, sir,' he said shyly, looking at Jonah for support.

'Do you get ill with them? Do they bother you in any way?'

'No, sir; sometimes I had a little stomach pain but that's due to green mangoes, sir.'

Dr Kawa put the stethoscope to his ears and moved the bell end over Kamara's chest with smooth delicate movements, while Kamara breathed deeply through his mouth. Then he squeezed his tummy, put the stethoscope back on the table, and examined Saidu's teeth, throat and the back of his ears.

'You look sound and healthy enough, but we must get rid of those worms for you. Run along now, and we'll tell you what to do later.' He made a note on Kamara's form.

'Do you hear much through the stethoscope, sir?' Jonah asked when Saidu had gone to send in the next boy. Kawa chuckled.

'Not very much, but as the lawyer wears a wig, and the priest a collar, so the doctor must have a stethoscope. It's a symbol. People believe in it; it gives them confidence, and the doctor as well.' The next boy arrived. 'How many more have I got to see?' he asked.

71

'Three hundred. Can't you come again tomorrow? It's a lot for one day,' Jonah said.

'No, tomorrow I have to be at the hospital. Officially I'm supposed to see all three hundred boys by one o'clock, since it's my afternoon off.'

'You'll never get through, sir,' Jonah ventured. They laughed together like colleagues.

Soon Dr Kawa was obliged to ask fewer questions of the boys to speed up his examinations. By midday he was yawning and had seen a hundred boys.

'I shan't know what I'm about, if I go on at this rate,' he said. They squeezed in another forty before lunch.

'Ah, here we are. Let me introduce you, starting with the familiar faces,' Mr Hamilton said, resting his glass of sherry on the table as they entered his office. 'I don't need to introduce you to Mr McGregor, still the backbone of our Science block.' Mr McGregor was an unsmiling but good-humoured Scot with an acid, frank tongue and sharp inquisitive blue eyes. He dressed shabbily on principle and when he was not picking his nose, he was digging his fingers into his anal cleft. His life spent in the Tropics, he had become something of an institution and a large part of the heart of the school. He was proud of his Highland accent which he put on specially at every opportunity because he was afraid of losing it.

'Aye, Ah remember the wee lad. Is this no' the lad that couldna dissect a frog, because the frog kept looking at him?' He shook hands, grimacing uninhibitedly.

'It's very nice to see some old faces left,' Dr Kawa said.

'D'ye hear him? Old faces he says. Now he is a doctor right enough. D'ye cut or sew, Doctor? Aye, we don't hear much out here, but we gather things, and I thought the same chap was no' allowed to cut the patient and sew him up again.'

'Still very sharp ears as well as eyes, Mr McGregor,' Dr Kawa replied laughing.

'Call me Gregory. Have you read the latest book by Thomas Mann? Ye haven't? Well, Gregory or Gregorius is the offspring of an incestuous concubinage . . . the story of Moses all over again . . .' He dropped his accent suddenly and assumed an air of seriousness as he continued 'but he becomes the greatest Pope that ever lived. I, sir, am the Holy Sinner. But don't take any notice. That's just to show my colleagues, who think that as a scientist I don't appreciate the "softer" things in life, but I do. Now don't take me off the subject. You doctors, you don't have a trade union or some such blasted thing?'

'We don't have a trade union yet,' Dr Kawa said joining in the mirth which had spread round the room.

'Indeed! It hasn't swallowed you yet.'

'I rather think we'd stick in its throat.'

'Well, anyway, welcome home,' Mr McGregor said suddenly, dropping his mask and clasping Dr Kawa warmly on both shoulders.

Mr Hamilton continued his introductions.

'Mr Duncan came to us from the Grammar School via Trinity College, Dublin, and does Mathematics. Miss Johnson does Languages.' Dr Kawa shook hands as Mr Hamilton went on to explain that Miss Johnson had introduced French into the curriculum in addition to Latin, and that it was proving a success.

'Now, how about some sherry?' he asked Dr Kawa, indicating to Jonah to get some. When he had armed Dr Kawa with a glass, Mr Hamilton raised his.

'Well, here's to you,' he said, and they put their glasses to their lips, murmuring some kind of toast.

73

'I hope you did not have too bad a morning,' Mr Hamilton said, already refilling his glass.

'I'm afraid efficiency declined towards the end.'

'Too many boys, eh? Some hundred and fifty more than when you were here I should think.'

'Fortunately not many sick ones,' Dr Kawa said.

'Good, good. Things have changed you know.'

'Quite a few with a variety of intestinal worms, I fear.'

'I know. Your predecessor was of the opinion that unless you get hold of the rest of their families and thrash theirs out as well, it is a waste of time treating the boys in isolation.' Mr Hamilton had a way of emphasizing some words which made you think he had his tongue in his cheek.

'That, I suppose, is just about it,' Dr Kawa said hesitantly.

'Still, we must do what we can,' Mr Hamilton concluded as he moved away and made room for Mr McGregor who had become alerted by the subject of worms, and had joined the other two with an expression of surreptitious intimacy on his face. He spoke in Dr Kawa's ear, but none too softly.

'I say, if you ever find the answer to "Lumbricus" do let me know. I've had them for twenty years you know . . . generations of them.' He looked round the room as if he did not wish to be overheard, but really to make certain that everyone was listening. 'The "Hook" – the one that looks like a Mende devil – got him too. Would miss them now really, but they're so damned itchy. Drive me crazy sometimes; and these damned boys. They notice, you know.' He broke off the intimacy suddenly and assumed the air of one affronted. 'And don't I remember you imitating me once, some thirteen years ago, yourself?'

74

'You've got a better memory than I,' Dr Kawa replied. McGregor looked towards Miss Johnson who was talking to Mr Duncan. 'Now there's another thing that drives me crazy, and one you did not expect to find here, I'm sure. Female members of staff in a man's school.'

'Are you on your hobby-horse again, Mr McGregor?' Miss Johnson said good-humouredly, turning round abruptly. 'He doesn't approve of me; or pretends not to,' she said to Dr Kawa.

'Well, what about that for a lie. My disapproval as you call it has nothing whatever to do with you as a person – you know I'm very fond of you. It's the principle. Women are everywhere except in bed these days, which is where they ought to be.' Undaunted by the fact that all eyes were fixed on him, he looked sternly at Jonah. 'Principal, may I suggest that we send the laddie out of the room? Grown men ought to be able to speak their minds without being spied on . . . not that you can teach them very much these days.'

'Perhaps his presence will remind us to moderate our enthusiasm,' Mr Hamilton replied with suppressed delight. Mr McGregor waved his arms, shrugged and pretended to sulk but did not forget what he had been saying.

'If you young men don't stand up for yourselves, Africa is finished, and I speak sincerely. Speaking as a friend of Africa – I've almost become an African over the years, worse luck!'

'The situation sounds grave,' Dr Kawa said.

'Grave, he says. That's where the whole damn lot is heading for.'

'So what do you . . .' Dr Kawa began.

'Ah! So what do you suggest we do about it, you're going to ask. Well, that's a question your grandfather would never have thought of asking. What do I suggest you do? Keep them as women, of course. Mind you, I don't mean keep them down. Oh no! But first and foremost, keep them as women. Insist on it. Twenty years ago, when I came out to Africa, there were great men in this Continent, and Africa was great and full of promise – never mind the bloody Imperialists. Now we are asked to think in terms of great women. What nonsense.' A burst of laughter brightened the room.

'You may laugh,' Mr McGregor went on assuming a declamatory style. 'Take the Roman Empire. What was the scoundrel's name? Livia? Livia. She started Rome's decline. And France. When the women started shouting for power, the men had had enough of it anyway and were only too happy to step down and give way, and with them the State.' He stopped and cleared his throat.

'All this is ancient history really,' Dr Kawa said.

'So you want modern parallels. I'll give them to you. Take the United States – America. They may have all the luxury and nuclear bombs and what have you, but they are in a state of moral decline, and the reason is that the soil has lost its humus. The women have dug their feet out of the rich bubbling soil and want to be in the White House and in executive positions. Some can't even breast-feed their children without a book to tell them how to do it. All very nice; but you can't produce a virile posterity without a soul, and that is what happens when women abandon their fundamental function in life, and I am sorry to confess that the once greatest nation in the world, planted on that sceptred isle, is running an easy second. Women are differently made from men – you can't get away from that – at least they used to be when I had any dealings with them. It's no use pretending they're not. They think differently and they react differently. You might as well believe you can fertilize yourself. Now I don't know about you, but I have had the misfortune of being involved in accidents with both men drivers and women. The man sees danger approaching, and may even know that escape is impossible but he tries to turn the wheel, or perhaps swerve away from the poor pedestrian on the pavement. The woman shuts her eyes until she comes round in hospital, if she's lucky.' There was a gasp of relief from Miss Johnson.

'An interesting theory, but we've a long way to go before women carve out our spines in Africa,' Dr Kawa said.

'Beware of the subtle black goddesses, young man, because when they get hold of what they call privileges, you won't be able to distinguish it from power hunger, and make no mistake, women love power even more than men. These goddesses will carve out your spine as you say, while you are making love to them. Here, my one and last ambition; to start a suffragette movement . . . for Men of Africa, before it is too late.' He finished his sherry, draining the very last drop, and put the glass on the tray. He was obviously very pleased with his oration and was sweating freely.

'Give a wee thought to what I have said, my boy, and remember: if it takes you a quarter of the time to absorb the Western civilization as it took to knock it together, it will only take you one twentieth of the time to lose your soul; and once that's gone, finished; eaten up.' He lumbered over to Miss Johnson and putting his arm through hers, walked her to the door.

'Thank you, Principal – God Bless,' he said as they went out arm in arm.

'Those two seem to share an odd pleasure in antagonism,' Mr Hamilton commented as he led Dr Kawa towards the south window, and pulled the curtain back so that they could see across the bay. There Mr Duncan joined them.

'You were at Cambridge, I believe,' Mr Duncan began.

'Yes, for the first part of my training, then of course I had to go to a London hospital.'

'How long for?'

'Three years.'

'What college?'

'Trinity.'

'Interesting; I went to Trinity, Dublin. The two places have a lot in common, you know.'

'I've never been to Dublin though I always meant to. Beautiful place, I gather,' Dr Kawa replied.

'Ireland's all right. The Irish are friendly and of course it's cheaper than Cambridge; but the Colleges are similar.'

'Historically?'

'No . . . I believe you have a large court?'

'Yes; Great Court – said to be one of the largest in England.'

'We also have a large court in Dublin; you see apart from that the traditions are similar.'

'When did you visit Cambridge?' Dr Kawa asked.

'Actually I never had time to go there. Preferred London you know! But one gathers things.'

The three men were looking over the sheer drop of the promontory on which the school stood, across the calm water of Kroo Bay, towards the rugged cliffs on the opposite side with its scattered assortment of buildings, shops, offices and shacks, and on the far side of the ledge, the old grey stone of the hospital. Towering behind it was a five-storied Lebanese mansion with a sun roof; grotesque in its setting, hideously bare and unadorned.

It had stopped raining and the sun was stark naked. Small fishing boats were setting out from the bay, and in the distance two cargo ships were steaming out of port.

'Good site Yor a hospital, don't you think?' Mr Hamilton observed.

'Excellent view, but rather close to the edge,' Dr Kawa rejoined.

'Pity! It leaves so little room for expansion.'

'It's very cramped at present. I understand there is a plan afoot for moving across Water Street and expanding inwards, as it were.'

'That has been afoot for years, but nobody can persuade the owner of the land to sell, and the powers that be have not dared to make a compulsory purchase yet,' Mr Duncan said with some heat.

'They'll have to do something pretty soon,' Dr Kawa said.

'These Lebanese come and make all the money by fair means or foul, yet they won't make any sacrifices for the country,' Mr Duncan said.

'Well, there's a job for you. Start leaving your mark on the Service, get the pawns moving,' Mr Hamilton said to Dr Kawa.

The school bell rang hoarsely through the building. The two men sat at the small table for lunch while Mr Duncan finished his drink and excused himself.

'Not a bad crowd; quite happy.' Mr Hamilton said when Mr Duncan had left.

'Seems to know a lot about Cambridge for someone who has never seen the place,' Dr Kawa observed.

'That young man typifies the attitude of our young men today. It's a reaction to frustration, to bitterness, lack of opportunity and insecurity. They try to get round it all by pretending to know everything and to be what they are not. To prove they are as good as the next man. Only a passing phase.'

Jonah set the dishes on the table and was dismissed. He had ten minutes in which to get his lunch.

*   *   *   *

The examinations continued all the afternoon, and it was 5.30 p.m. when Dr Kawa got up from his chair. He was genuinely pleased with the help Jonah had given him, and Jonah was thrilled to have given it. They said good-bye, and Jonah watched him go down the drive and out until his car disappeared round a corner, where the school boundary merged into the multi-coloured aluminium roofed houses of King Toms.

The sun was setting beyond the left haunch of Lion Mountain, and the pale sunset was beginning to burst open the blooms of the lily which crowded the margins of the forecourt. Far away in the hilly distance, Jonah could see figures climbing sinuous paths towards the smoke fires of Gloucester.

Chapter Six

The following weeks sank into the nursery of memory before Dr Kawa was aware of their passing. His days were well filled, professional activities soaking up the remains of energy which the sun had not wrung out of him. The more he grew outwardly in stature the emptier he felt within. He was alone in a unique sense. All his values and preferences appeared to cut across those of the people around him. Often he had wanted to talk to his mother about things, and she had been waiting for him to open his heart to her, but the fear that she might not understand sealed his lips and the torment within him.

He had kept away from clubs and refused as many social invitations as discretion allowed, and on those evenings when he was off duty and a restlessness began to creep under his skin, he would leave the house, walk a little way down the road, and across Congo Bridge. Following a footpath to the right, he would walk beside the stream for hours until his mind and body were consummated in fatigue and then he would go home to bed.

One evening as he walked by the stream folded in his own thoughts he heard heavy footsteps running towards him and before he could get out of the way, two boys bumped into him, nearly knocking him over, and fled in the direction from which he had come. It was too dark to see their faces but he thought that one was doing up his trousers as he ran. The sound of their heavy feet thundered into silence. A few yards farther on he heard a rustling in the reeds and a low whimpering. At first he took no notice of it, as he was used to the presence of wild goats in the area, but even in the dark he could see that the reeds on his left had been broken. The whimper became the sound of crying. Dr Kawa moved towards the sound, kicking against the clodded roots of reeds which might have been uprooted by a violent storm. A few yards off the path he saw the figure of a girl trying to pick herself and her clothes off the ground. She was crying so intensely that she had not heard his approach. When she became aware of his presence she was so frightened that she could not scream. She threw herself away from him against the reeds like a terrified animal and he could hear her shaking like a leaf.

'No more; please, *please!*' she whispered helplessly, and fell back in a faint.

Dr Kawa knelt beside her. She was cold and her teeth chattered violently. He put his coat round her and felt for some matches in his pocket and lit one. She was young. He rescued the tattered remnants of her pants from a reed, lifted her with infinite care, first resting her on his knee, and began to carry her home. He recognized the sticky feel of blood from her skirt on his hand. Instinctively he avoided the road and forded the stream beyond the bridge from where he scrambled his way home.

He laid her on his bed and kept her warm and sat himself in a chair beside her. He felt completely paralysed and could not think what was the right thing to do. Thoughts of ringing the police occurred to him. The word rape hammered at his brain. They were in darkness, she on the bed and he in the chair. He was strangely fascinated by her breathing. Soon she regained some consciousness and stretched out a hand to touch him.

'Where am I?' she whispered.

Dr Kawa took her hand, holding it tight. 'You're all right. You're safe,' he said.

The dim shadows of memory seemed to convulse her and she became restless, tossing her head from side to side in a frenzy and breathing heavily as if fighting for her life.

'Oh God, Oh God, why should this happen to me?'

Dr Kawa listened in silence for a while, letting her anguish pour out while she was yet insensible of the pains. Her hand grew warmer in his.

'Where am I?' she persisted.

'You're safe. I found you,' he said. Silence. She gulped. 'Did you stop them? I mean . . . did . . .'

'I was too late,' he whispered.

'Who are you?' she asked.

'My name is Kawa. I'm a doctor.'

'I've heard about you,' she said.

'What's your name?' he asked.

'Laura,' she replied as if in the half-light of sleep.

The name touched Dr Kawa strangely. He went to the window and drew deep on the honeysuckle sweet air. An emotional vacuum seemed to open between them and they were drawn towards each other. He wanted to see her, touch her. He turned on the table light. Even in the circumstances, she seemed to him pumpkin fresh. Her eyes were large, black, unspeaking, and she had something of the bloom clinging to rose petals. She forced a smile which brought dimples to her cheeks. A gap between her top front teeth under an apologetic nose seemed a breach in her defences. Her skin was soft, tight and clear as cobweb. She was black and beautiful without overtones of shade; like freshly burnt charcoal on the plains.

'How do you feel?' he asked.

'How should I feel? I have not been raped before,' she said firmly, and almost immediately burst into tears. Still crying she swung herself out of the bed. Dr Kawa sat beside her and held her shaking shoulders.

'I must go home now,' she said.

'I'll take you home and get in touch with the police,' he said. Laura suddenly stopped crying and cast a watery glance at him.

'I must go alone and nobody is to hear about this,' she said.

'But you can't let them get away with it,' he said angrily.

'I can if I want to.'

'Did you . . . did you know them?' he blurted out, moulding one fist into his palm.

'No. I never saw them before.'

'But we must report this,' he insisted.

'What difference will it make?' she said.

*   *   *   *

That night Dr Kawa did not sleep and for days afterwards his life centred around thoughts of Laura. In the confusion of his emotions he had not even remembered to ask her address. Often as he drove on his rounds he would find himself scrutinizing everyone who might be Laura. But he wondered if his feelings were not merely the result of his own loneliness and his pity for her experience.

One hot afternoon he was relaxing after lunch when there was a knock at the door. He opened the door with an expression of surprise and recollection at the caller.

'Jonah,' he said, testing his own memory.

'Yes, sir. I'm sorry to bother you.'

'Come in. What's the matter?'

Jonah walked timidly into the sitting-room and stood with his hands fidgeting in front of him.

'Sit down,' Dr Kawa said.

'Thank you sir. This won't take long.'

'Well, what's the trouble?' Dr Kawa asked sympathetically. Jonah did not know how to begin and fumbled for words. 'It's not me. There is nothing wrong with me. Actually my parents don't know anything about it. Even she doesn't know that I have come to see you.'

'You can trust me to keep a secret. It's part of my job,' Dr Kawa said, trying to put him at his ease.

'It's my sister, sir. I was wondering if you would see her if . . . if I can persuade her to come, sir.'

'Of course. But won't your sister come if she's ill?'

'She isn't exactly ill, sir. But she has not been herself for many weeks now, and I am worried about her.'

'Perhaps you would like to bring her to the hospital, say next Friday. About six in the evening. I have usually seen most of the patients by then.'

'Thank you, sir,' Johan said, getting up to go. 'I'll try to persuade Laura to come.'

'*Laura*?'

'Yes, sir.'

*　　*　　*　　*

So they came together again. Dr Kawa entered into a world of happiness which he had not known existed. Laura was in her first spring of love but the harshness of her rape still hung like black clouds on the horizon of a clear sky. She loved him but could not yet involve her body and he respected her reluctance. He tried to be unselfish in his love; hers, he knew, was tinged with hate.

The rushing days which overtook them were honey-dripping and mad like the green rushes by the brook where they sometimes sang to a knowing moon. They nestled by night under the Cotton Tree majesty of the open spaces, when the lights of Freetown had gone out.

On Thursday evenings he waited for her by the Law Courts and she would come hurrying up the avenue from the Cathedral, where she attended confirmation classes, and they would take the bus to Lumley Beach.

Feathered by the intoxicating freshness of salt air they would walk several miles along the sea front to the cape where they linked tongues and bruised noses at the foot of the old lighthouse. Then when the sun lowered her sail and the strain of the glittering ocean lifted from their eyes, they would follow the changing wind through ankle-deep sands and under tall coconut trees and open palms to a stretch of beach where they would watch a whole phalanx of crabs disappear in an instant in the wake of receding waves. With minutes to lose they would break through the reeds which fringed the Lake of Aberdeen, and would run down to the swaying jetty to catch the ferry, the diamond sparkle of Laura's laugh ringing in his ears. Cramped by the silence of the other passengers, Laura would sit on his knees as the ferryman wafted them across on the yesterbound vessel of his ballads.

His songs crystallized in Dr Kawa's memory. He it was who had ferried the great chief Zimba to the three-cornered island which lifts its head from the bottom of the lake at the moon-shifting hour of midnight, when the great fish of the ocean had sucked away the water for the great cleansing of the Sea God. . . . That Zimba who had renounced his stool and had trafficked with the gods in the forlorn hope of finding a faithful woman.

The old man sang languid songs to the other passengers in the high-pitched voice of a bat's squeak, his shoulders arched over the punt pole and his broad feet gripping the bottom of the boat. Then turning to the lovers, his eyes would twinkle and he would feather the water with his pole and sing a love ballad, opening his mouth so widely that they saw the red fragments of chewed cola sticking to his palate.

Then when they reached the other bank he would refuse the fares, saying that if he could ferry a star across the lake every day of his life, he would ask nothing more. Instead Laura would curtsy awkwardly to him before they scrambled up the stony path and caught the bus back to Brookfield.

There, in front of the recreation grounds, they would buy some food, stewed liver and bread wrapped in old newspapers, under the flickering light of kerosene lamps and the chatter of crickets, then plunge among the rushes on the opposite hillside not far from where they had first met, and, breaking the flow of the brook with their feet, they would picnic. Often Laura would fall asleep in his arms to the humming of distant drums from over the hills, falling on their ears as soft-footed as the wild goats which came to share their sky-vaulted retreat.

Laura grew more beautiful under the warmth of their intimacy and even her slight limp, the result of an illness in childhood, had become oddly attractive to him.

But all their days were not cloudless. The memory of her rape would sometimes surge to the surface and Laura would be inconsolable. At such times she would be taciturn, tearful and would even refuse to see Dr Kawa for days on end. They had promised never to talk about that first meeting, but both understood that it was loneliness which had driven them both on those nightly walks which for her had ended tragically.

*　　*　　*　　*

Kissy Street was already throbbing with pleasure seekers and between infrequent lamp-posts the numerous wine and spirit bars cast their lights across the street. High Life and jazz streamed from the windows, and groups of drummers with their followers held up the traffic from time to time.

Freetown by night had always fascinated Dr Kawa. The atmosphere was alive and electric – music, shouting from the bars, good humour, smashing bottles, bicycle bells ringing, drums and swearing pedestrians. It usually made his heart light but he had no taste for it as he sped over the road bridges which straddled the gutters.

He left his car by the sub-police station at Fourah Bay Road and half ran down a narrow lane to the left, guiding himself along the railing. On his left the waters of the precipitous gorge poured between slanted concrete shelves like a waterfall. At the bottom of the lane he went down a few steps and on to a platform. Here the lane swung sharply to the right and became an alleyway of soft red earth. He turned right along the road. Somewhere in the distance he could hear the roaring of the sea. He quickened his steps past the Fulani trader who sold cigarettes, matches and gunpowder from a tin cage at the street corner by candlelight.

Softly past the low-roofed palm-wine bars and the peripheral fortress of stone houses where odours of herbs of every description, roots and barks of trees filled the air. He was penetrating the heart of Soldier Town, so named because it contained the shady grottoes which soldiers from Tower Hill Barracks frequented. It was said that murders were not investigated in that part of the town, since the nearby gorge with its rushing waters served as an efficient and dumb accomplice.

The lanes now wound in and out between the houses and over a network of drains. They twisted and turned, divided and rejoined, but Dr Kawa skilfully negotiated the labyrinths and swimming through the heavy smell of sweat and wet earth suddenly found himself in an open square.

The square was crowded with people, mostly soldiers, drunk and sober. At the far end a group of people danced in gay abandon, one girl twisting her spine backwards in a perfect curve until her head touched the sand. A masquerade was disappearing down a lane to the right. The air vibrated with human life.

Dr Kawa ran diagonally across the square, escaping from the crowds into a narrow lane. He hurried down the lane which brought him to a circle of six thatched huts with an orange tree at the centre. All the huts were in darkness except one from which a light shone through the bottom of the door. An elderly man in a white khaftan about to begin his prayers sat on a mat outside one of the huts, dexterously washing his feet from a kettle by suspending them in the air in turn. A woman washed her infant behind another hut.

Dr Kawa stopped under the orange tree to catch his breath and collect his thoughts. He felt his damp vest sticking to his skin and he pulled it away with finger and thumb so that his chest was fanned by a cool gust of air. Now that he had come all this way he was uncertain what he was going to do or say. He moved towards the lighted door and noticed his hands were trembling. The door was unlocked. He opened it and stood immediately in a barely-furnished room. A soft light burned. Laura lay on a low bed, her arm stretched out and her fingers wrapped round the neck of a palm-wine-bottle. She was naked to the waist. In a state of exhaustion a young man sat in a chair admiring her breasts.

Dr Kawa stood rooted for a few moments. At first Laura did not see him, then she opened her eyes slowly, recognized him and gasped.

'Who told you?' she mouthed drunkenly.

'I received an unsigned letter,' he replied.

'I am sorry. I am going to have a baby,' she blurted out. The young man looked on sheepishly and uncomprehendingly.

Summoning up all her energy, she raised herself off the bed. Much as he wanted to take her hand, perhaps to swear forgiveness, he could not move. The ground under his feet had suddenly become a chasm into which the concentration of all he valued had been swept away in a single irremediable instant. He left them together without another word.

Chapter Seven

Windswept October came to moderate the September storms which had raged over the countryside. In the bulge which formed the haunch of Lion Mountain a crust of earth undermined by the rains had slid down the valley causing great loss of life. The amateurishly conducted rescue operations were further hindered by politicians who seized yet another opportunity of spreading the mudbaths of September downpours. Freetown and the entire Peninsula moaned under grey skies and mouthed prayers to the churning winds. Down in Kroo Bay the clustered shacks of tin and wood stood pathetically like ravaged vultures with their feet washed by the overflowing stream. The colourfully painted figures on their walls and roofs had already been washed away by the rain, leaving only the macerated remnants of colour from the previous year. The black and white days of summer's glory had toned down into a mood of sombre and persistent greyness, and the skirts of the Harmatan – the cold dry desert wind – brushed over the earth and sowed sharp needles in the air.

Dr Kawa had not seen or heard from Laura. The shock of his first real emotional awakening had affected him strangely. The love which was the basis of their relationship remained and tormented him more through dreams than in conscious thought. One evening as he lay on his couch watching the stars of early evening through the window he fell asleep and dreamed.

He had gone to meet Laura at Tower Hill at her request. It had been one of their favourite walks. As he waited, he repeated to himself some lines he had written.

> *Come dredge this Oasis of love*
> *On whose waters no thirst has been quenched*
> *Since we both dipped our young lips*
> *In its clear reflection, Moorish on our knees.*

With his fingers he squeezed out the oil of a eucalyptus leaf. Teased by the eloquence of honeysuckle and magnolia blossoms, he did not recognize Laura when she first appeared at the bottom of the avenue. She hesitated in the glow of frescoed light then leaning forward leaped off the mark as if to run up the hill, but stopped herself quite suddenly and walked towards him with slow deliberate steps. It was the piquant twist of her body towards her left hip when she tried to hurry which lit up the old fascination and prompted his recognition.

She seemed more mature, more beautiful as she approached with her hands in the pockets of her brown corduroy coat. It was a look he had not seen before and for a while he let its meaning flounder on the rock of his indifference.

'Well?' he said firmly.

'How are you?' Laura asked with a forced smile. In the poor light he could see the lines of her mouth trembling and the tenseness of her eyes relaxing. Suddenly he felt pained and did not want her to cry. His love for Laura had been warped, bruised and tortured; it had been disguised by jealousy, hate, pride and mistrust, but it was still alive.

'You look well,' he said unevenly. A tear broke on her collar.

'Are you in a hurry?' she asked, not attempting to dry her face.

'No, not particularly,' he replied and automatically held the crushed eucalyptus leaf to her nose. She turned her head away and ran to the opposite row of trees, plucking a leaf herself. She stood with her back to him sniffing at the leaf and he knew she was sobbing. He moved towards her.

'Shall we walk?' she said at length when she had dried her face.

They walked hand in hand to the top of the road where the avenue came to an abrupt end and the road levelled to form a ledge on the hillside; the granite rocks rose vertically to the barracks of red brick on the summit. To the right the closely cropped grass like a green carpet overlooked the western end of the city. The wind had died down and the air was warm. As he helped Laura down the foot drop from the road on to the path which meandered between the meadows down and round the base of Tower Hill, the sun blinked and it was night. Down and round they walked towards a place where a granite bench had been carved out of the hillside. There they sat like dispossessed monarchs on their throne, separated by silence.

'What is it?' he asked, clasping her hand, his mind filled with premonition.

'I have not come to ask your forgiveness. I know that is impossible,' Laura began. He felt the steady maturity in her voice; a voice sustained by full sentences and no longer mouse-bitten and childishly incoherent.

'I told you once that love should be based on friendship,' she said, paused and withdrew her hand from beneath his. 'It is as a friend that I come to you now.'

He longed to learn the truth about what had come between them; that she was innocent of connivance towards their desolation. His yearning cried out for her exculpation, yet he was afraid. Afraid of the ever present possibility of seeing magnified that molecule of doubt which had so juggled his reason. Laura eased his conscience a little but only after she had inflicted a moment of such intense sorrow as to cause him physical pain.

'I need your help,' she said.

'What is it?'

'I'm pregnant.'

He got up and stamped wildly on the rock shelf on which they perched. The earth moved from under him for a second time and he felt himself hovering in space. With those words he realized that pain, like joy, was tiered in endless variety and unpredictability. When he was able to look at her again there was a hard lump where his heart should have been, but it was with tenderness and cool reason that he spoke.

'Does anyone else know about it?' he asked sitting beside her.

'No; only you and I.'

'No one else?' he insisted.

Laura understood his implication.

'You don't think I want to see him ever again?'

'But he's the father – isn't he?' he shouted in a moment of overwhelming hatred and despair.

Laura fell weeping away from him on the bench, and from the sting on his cheek he realized she had struck him.

'Don't let's hurt each other any more,' he said trying to lift her head. 'I was too wounded in my own feelings to know what you were going through. One drowning man cannot save another.'

She raised her body and rested her chin in her cupped hand. Her eyes were still wet and there was a sternness in her face. 'You were prepared to believe the most terrible thing about me without even wanting to know the truth?' she said.

The accusation seemed true and piercing.

'I'm sorry. If you knew how much I wanted to know the truth – but I was a coward and could not face it. What I saw was enough, Laura; anything more would have finished me.'

'You thought I was rotten,' she whispered, searching for his mouth with her fingers. He held her hand and they trembled in unison.

'No! No! I knew it was impossible . . . b-but there was always a doubt.'

Laura wrenched her hand away and began to sob more freely than before. 'It was so cruel; so mean and cruel, and I could not run away. I could do nothing. But I don't want even to think about it. If you knew what I'd been through – Oh God. But how can one make a man understand? How?' Laura covered her face with both hands and all but beat her head against the rock, gasping to alleviate the pain of her sobs.

'Now we've faced the worst we must expose everything,' he said.

'Tell everybody?' she asked startled, and straining to define his meaning from his face.

'No, Laura; not tell everybody: but we must leave no more doubts in our minds. We must expose our hearts once and for all.'

Laura had begun to weep again, continuously like the smooth running of an engine and burying her face in his breast when her recollections grew too painful. She took the fold of his chest muscle in her mouth as a cat lifts her kitten, safely and without injury, rolling her head from side to side. The warm trickle of her tears soaked through his shirt and made it stick to his skin. She stopped crying and raised her face to look at him, her face a luminous shadow in the grey October night.

He was choked by the futility of words. He struck his thighs again and again wishing there was some way in which he could wash her hands in the full cup of his heart – some way in which he could make her see his genuine shame. Shame for what? He longed for an act – words more noble and less paltry than 'I'm sorry.' The mere thought of the words angered him by their inadequacy. They lacked the quality of a final, irreversible vow of devotion. They were used as a mere stop-gap. They were meaningless because their backbone had dropped out during their hackneyed life. Should he make love to her? He had no such desire. Instead he kissed her deep in the furrows of her brow.

'What can I do? What can I do? What is to become of me? My family will disown me if I have the child. What can I do? The beast!' she cried. Instantly she seemed to be in a panic. Her cries echoed in the hollow of the rock in an uncanny way and his imagination constructed a Laura three years in the future; mother of a fatherless child, friendless, disowned, without an income or the means of earning one, and torn between infanticide and starvation on one hand, and infamous living on the other.

'We must expose him,' he said defiantly with the idealism of youth. 'A good thing is the right thing to do whatever the cost . . . at any rate our consciences will have been relieved.' Laura started violently as if there had been an explosion and clung to him. He felt her un-even breath on his face and saw that look of amiable and tolerant incredulity, which adults show to children, in her eyes. Then she twisted about vainly as she searched for words to express herself adequately. Finding none she contented herself with saying, 'I wanted to just disappear and find myself in another world where I could not remember anything; anything . . . I . . . I wanted to kill myself.'

'No Laura!' he said with a conviction that surprised him. 'Your life is infinitely more important than what happens to it.'

'I don't understand anything any more; just when I thought I did,' she said. 'God knows. I have only thought of saving you from shame. I could not do anything with-out seeing you.' She sighed and waited for her heart to stop racing. 'Not even kill myself.'

The words seemed to shine through the impenetrable darkness in which they sat like foetuses, and he experi-enced something that was more vital than life and death, though he had no idea what it was. He felt elevated, noble, and utterly selfless. He leant over and kissed her ear through the coils of hair.

'How you've grown these few months, Laura,' he said.

'Will you help me to get rid of the baby?' she asked, taking his hand hopefully.

'You must not even think of it,' he said.

'Please understand; please help me. There's no other way out. Do you think I have come to this decision easily?'

A silence followed during which neither seemed to breathe. It seemed like the moment in court when the jury are filing back with a man's life hanging from the foreman's tongue.

'We shall get married at once,' he said.

Laura threw her hand over his mouth with such force that he fell backwards, striking his head against the bare rock. She was shaking and her teeth chattered as when he had first met her among the reeds. He did not attempt to free himself but lay there waiting for her to speak. When she recoiled she fell almost lifeless on his lap like a snake which has sunk all its energy and poison into one decisive bite. He grooved his arm around her and spread his hand over her abdomen where the child lay.

'I came to you for help as a friend; not for pity,' she said lifting her head on unsteady shoulders.

'Don't let us be meaningless,' he said. 'Pride, honour, justice, integrity, common sense – all those words we once believed in we have seen used as toilet paper.'

'I would not have come to you . . . I never dreamt that you . . .' Her refusal angered him. He got up and walked round the little mountain copse.

'What's all this selfless noble-mindedness mean? What is it worth if magic lantern heroes can seize it from you and walk on it? Haven't we learnt our lesson? That we're walking in mud up to our throats, but whatever happens we've just got to keep walking till we are submerged or reach the open sea!'

'Don't shout, please,' she said with narcotic gentleness and taking his hand she forced him to sit down. 'What you suggest is impossible,' she said.

'I know it is the right thing to do, and I am doing it because I need you. Because together we can prove ourselves stronger than events.'

His heart was beating faster with the effort of speaking. She buried her lips in his neck but not with the sweet kindliness of her playful moments nor the piercing granting of her passions. It was a kiss which made a statement;

whose casuistry declared with eloquent solemnity, '*How can I make you understand?*'

Suddenly Laura seemed to take on an ephemeral consistency and began to float away from him. Slowly she was swallowed up into the dark distance. He woke up sweating and straining to grasp her.

Someone was knocking at the door. He got up and shook his head into wakefulness, passed his fingers through his hair, straightened his trousers and went to the window. He looked out into the darkness and met the bright green eyes of a cat staring back from under the hedge. 'Hm,' he said, returning to his couch, thinking he had been mistaken. But before he reached it the unmistakable soft knock was repeated. He went to the door and opened it.

A figure swaying uneasily stood outside. While Dr Kawa tried to recognize who it was, the figure removed its hat and began to feel its way through the door.

'Jonah! You're drunk.'

'You're telling me,' Jonah slurred. His eyes seemed to rotate in their sockets as he fell flat on his back, bringing up some stomach contents on impact.

Dr Kawa put him to bed and mopped up the pool of vomit on the carpet. Then he put out the lights and went to the City Hotel for supper. When he returned Jonah was on his knees trying to clean up the marks that still showed on the carpet. He stood with a wet rag in his hand and looked the picture of horror.

Feeling better for his meal, Dr Kawa was anxious to put Jonah at his ease, and patted him on the shoulder.

'I didn't think you'd wake till morning,' he said. 'Put that thing away,' he added, pointing to the rag, 'and come and sit down.' Jonah obeyed in silence. He sat on the edge of the chair with his head between his knees.

'I'm sorry, sir. I'm so ashamed,' he said.

'You had one too many. Often I feel like it myself,' Dr Kawa replied. Jonah looked full in Dr Kawa's face with his damp appealing eyes. They had got to know something of each other over the months during the time of the liaison between Dr Kawa and Laura. Dr Kawa saw a thousand questions in his look.

'What is it, Jonah?' he asked.

'She's gone; she's disappeared. We don't know what's happened to her,' he said.

'She has good reason for wanting to get away, Jonah. Don't blame her too much. She will come back in her own time.'

'I know about it. She is going to have a baby. But why run away? Who will look after her? Why?' he screamed and could not go on.

'You were fond of her too!'

'I loved her. I loved her when we were children, and I still love her. She is the only woman I have ever loved; my sister.' Jonah said with triumphant defiance.

Dr Kawa stood with his mouth open. His throat was parched and he could not speak. Jonah got up and looked for his hat, found it and went to the door. As he opened it he looked back.

'I love her as a man loves a woman,' he said and disappeared into the darkness.

Chapter Eight

The bitter wind shall not crumble the reed. The year turned its back on the fruits which had not ripened with summer, fruits that would never lose the sun-yellow pride of their immaturity or the pale sour pulp round the healthy seed. December changed slyly into a new year and soon the April weather blossomed like a flower.

The drought was yet to come in that erupting year of uncertainties and controversies which began with a threat that the Christmas celebrations would continue into Easter. In April the sun was on its northbound journey from the Tropic of Capricorn and Freetown basked in the pleasant coolness of its shadow.

Political events flared across Africa like a trail of gunpowder, and even those who survived the shock waves did not avoid having their fingers burnt. The paddy fields of politics were flooded up and down the country with poisoned water, and a climate was created in which everyone was expected to become involved. Any who remained neutral were labelled 'stooge', 'traitor', 'nonpatriot'.

A new constitution had been designed at last to inculcate the principles of democratic government whereby the majority groups up-country would be allowed a greater say in the hitherto minority influenced legislature. The people of Freetown were baffled by this gratuity from their rulers. For one thing they had absorbed fully and without due reflection the principle that 'corn grows at the expense of rain and sunlight,' and they, of course, were the corn. But they were puzzled by the sudden change of face of an administration which had for three centuries shrewdly and assiduously scuttled the cargoes of understanding and mutual respect between the 'Protected' and 'Colonial' peoples of Sierra Leone and had now unceremoniously decided to crack their heads together.

The social migraine which followed the advance guards of mistrust and corruption did not make for easy implementation of the constitution, and left a hangover more devastating than anything they had known before. If the people of Freetown had always suspected that the British were not to be trusted, they now believed that truth and virtue did not exist, and had never existed.

'Teething troubles,' shouted one.

'Chronic sinuses,' another.

'Teething troubles following extraction,' cried a solitary voice of cynicism which was promptly silenced.

It was felt that the contemplative English neither embraced nor rejected the affections of their Colonial people, but, like the doctor who examined his African patients with a bamboo pole, merely tolerated the disgust they inspired while rubbing the sweat off their brows with hooked fingers. Having provided a code of law and a modicum of education embellished with pious helpings of religious doctrine, they had nothing more to give. Yet if ignorance, barbarism, disease and pestilence had been halted there still remained the restless spirit of man which far from being harnessed, had been unleashed and neglected. The African did not know what was to become of him. Unwittingly he had bartered his soul for material gain. He had lost a good deal of his heritage in the process yet had not been fully admitted into the closely-guarded traditions of his rulers.

For all her bestial beginnings, colonial rule might have set Africa herself solidly on a road towards a new civilization. But what was to be done now? How to breathe under water? How save a sinking ship? How avoid the infection of the great powers – the sugar candy powers? How did one educate the many without resources? How to love without jealousy?

* * * *

While great national controversies raged, Dr Kawa's mind inclined towards a peaceful hibernation. He buried himself in his work to overcome the still painful memory of Laura. Often he sought his mother's sympathy – a sympathy of silence. He had admired her lack of opposition during his days with Laura, and returned her understanding with affection. Even when the end came, an end which sowed in him the feelings of inadequacy and guilt, she had offered comfort in her silence; she had not lectured him or talked about marriage, and this he was grateful for. With Laura he had found something he sought; a poetic expression of feeling, the symbol of a noble idea; this, he thought, meant more than a conventional marriage or procreation. But he had had much farther to fall.

* * * *

During his 'Laura period' as he came to think of those days, he had seen a good deal of Mr Marshall, and Sonia had become attached to him. He had avoided meeting Mrs Marshall, especially when the break came with Laura, because, in an odd way, he felt they were morally alike, and this irked him. In Mr Marshall he had observed an insidious change of personality.

Mr Marshall had come to assume a degree of intimacy which Dr Kawa had not always felt either existed or was necessary. For a time Mr Marshall had doted on Dr Kawa's relationship with Laura with an air of nostalgia, as if it had been his own and when Laura left the scene he had become almost dependent. He would drop in for a chat at odd hours of the day or night, and if Dr Kawa happened to be out Mr Marshall would sit, dozing with an open book on his knees, sometimes until the early hours of the morning, when the Doctor would return and find him there.

On a warm May evening when he could not stay at home and read, Dr Kawa wandered down to the Odeon Cinema.

Just before the interval he slipped out to the bar for a drink where he met Mr Hamilton.

'Hello, Kawa; come and have a drink with me,' Mr Hamilton greeted him. The two men had not met for a long time, and Dr Kawa felt hesitant at having to break the gap of so many months with a few moments of conversation.

'Hello,' he said. 'I'll have a brandy please. How do you like the film?' he asked while the brandy was being poured.

'Oh I don't come to watch films. I only drop in occasionally for a drink.'

The bar was already filling up.

'How's the school?' Dr Kawa asked self-consciously.

"Oh, all right; and you?'

'And I . . . ?' Dr Kawa repeated. 'Oh work . . . ups and downs.'

They drank without speaking for a while. The noise of

people commenting on the film and others ordering drinks had grown, and they were constantly being jogged by arms outstretched for glasses. Two stout men had riveted themselves to the bar and were staring fixedly at the barmaid. Mr Hamilton picked up his drink and, taking Dr Kawa by the arm, led him through the crowd to the quieter end of the room where they threw themselves into armchairs.

'I'm sorry I don't see more of you.' Mr Hamilton said.

'Partly work, partly reclusion,' Dr Kawa replied with a smile.

Mr Hamilton eyed him with interest. 'It's not my business, Kawa, but you know how news spreads. I can't pretend not to have heard.'

'At least I don't have to tell you, then,' Dr Kawa said.

'Of course you made a mistake; a selfish mistake. But who doesn't.'

Dr Kawa felt a pang at the words 'selfish mistake'. He had reproached himself so often for it but the words still held their sting. He mumbled into his glass.

Mr Hamilton continued, 'The thing is not to let mistakes get you down altogether. By the way, why don't you take up something to divert your mind from things?'

'What do you have in mind?'

'Anything; doesn't matter what it is.' After a pause Mr Hamilton added, 'Have you thought of taking an interest in politics for instance?'

'But I do take an interest,' Dr Kawa replied.

'More than an interest then. Nothing better to take you out of yourself.'

'Thanks, but I'm not ready for it. Perhaps later.'

Mr Hamilton smiled as if satisfied with having sown the seed in the other's mind. He got up and drained his glass.

'Well, I'm off to a political meeting. Much more amusing than films. Come and see me sometime; any time,' he said and waddled out.

The bell announcing the second half rang and the crowd began to move back to their seats, but Dr Kawa felt he could not sit through the rest of the film and walked towards the door. Outside Mr Marshall was examining the posters, debating whether to go in or not. He had not seen Dr Kawa come out and jumped when he was touched on the shoulder.

'Are you going in?' Dr. Kawa asked.

'Is it a serious film?' Mr Marshall wanted to know.

'Serious as films go. Why?'

'You see Clara doesn't like serious films so I can go to them without the fear of meeting her and being humiliated.'

'I'm going home,' Dr Kawa said.

'I think I'll come with you.'

Dr Kawa had left his car at home so Mr Marshall gave him a lift. They drove slowly up Westmoreland Street turning into Pademba Road at Cotton Tree. Mr Marshall stopped the car on Jockey Bridge and listened to the turbulent waters gurgling down to the sea. The stars shone steadily, not twinkling. He sighed deeply as he let the hand-brake off and moved on.

'Sonia has been asking about you. Wants to know why you don't come round. That child loves you as if you were her father.'

Dr Kawa woke from his contemplation and smiled wryly. A sudden wave of bitterness was taking hold of him and he did not speak. *It's unjust. There is no reason, no value, nothing.*

'I say Sonia is very fond of you,' Mr Marshall repeated.

His breathing was laboured. He opened the car window and sniffed greedily at the night air.

'Are you all right?' Dr Kawa asked.

'Oh yes, fine. Just a bit short of wind. I've noticed it recently. I'll be all right soon.'

'Shall we stop for a bit?' Dr Kawa asked. Just then Mr Marshall drove across some red lights without noticing them. Dr Kawa automatically thrust his foot down hard in a vain attempt to stop the car. A thin film of sweat moistened his skin. As they drove past a street lamp he noticed the dreamy look on Mr Marshall's face. His features looked drawn and old. It was like looking through a person at the disordered horror of his skeleton. Dr Kawa felt with a jolt that he was watching a man disintegrate under the imperceptible onslaught of age. But the process was also his own; it related to a totality. The potential of disintegration was profound and fearful.

'How are things at home?' he heard himself asking. Mr Marshall did not show surprise. He did not even move his head but answered from a cloudy detachment.

'She's not home just now.'

They turned round the bend and dipped down at the approach to Congo Bridge. The bridge lights flickered a hundred yards below. Down to the left Dr Kawa had first met Laura. Suddenly Mr Marshall put the brakes on hard. The car heaved forward so that the front bumper hit the road and sprang back. It swerved, lifting its near rear wheel on to the bank which guarded the deep fall into the stony waters below. Twisting and convulsing it came to a stop several yards downhill.

'What on earth . . .?' Dr Kawa muttered.

'Sorry. I . . . I thought I saw a body lying across the road. I saw it clearly. It was Clara and I did not . . .' He stopped talking and wiped the sweat off his brow.

They drove on in silence.

'Would you like to come turtle fishing?' Mr Marshall asked before they parted.

'Turtle fishing?' Dr Kawa repeated in surprise.

'Yes . . . it's great fun. Good night.'

Chapter Nine

About this time a migration of turtles had occurred from the margins of the Gambia River, where they had been harassed by the threat of extinction, into the sheltered bays which dotted the Freetown peninsula. Large numbers of these fugitives were to be seen floating south in the warm currents like a slowly moving reef glittering in the angled light on summer evenings. They sailed in desperate shoals down the curve of the African coast, driven by the death instinct against the unpredictability of wind and current. Daring the shark settlements, these aquatic nomads, homeless between the land and the sea, caught at the melting point of marine evolution, sought warm shelters for their eggs.

Mostly they stuck together in a convoy; but when the laying instinct became too strong they would turn their wrinkled necks and solemn eyes towards the beaches and the palms. In unprotected handfuls they would struggle up the sands still pulsating with yesterday's heat to deposit their eggs in dug out dark pouches of the earth. Then, exhausted by the mighty effort of procreation and clumsily shovelling the sand over their nests, they would lumber back to the sea, forgetting to cover their tracks. And when the sun lifted a weather-testing finger the turtles would raise their oyster heads above the shore-bound ripples and know that another year had expired.

There was nothing so inlaid with sadness as those haunted faces; a great sadness of tortured longevity.

But here too! Today as yesterday as the year before, death lurked in the pointed steel, the hoe and the beak. Death which gives permanence to life.

Hardly were the wet seeds rocked into place than the black ghosts descended from among the reeds armed with hoes and dug them up. Suddenly the beaches swarmed with excited villagers who filled their baskets with the turtle's eggs and left them to wash in the wake of the waves. Later they would salt them, spread them out on mats under the village sun until the yokes were brick-baked, and on damp evenings roast them on charcoal burners in their huts, filling the air with the warm charred smell of nuts as they ate them.

But for the turtles themselves fate was not so kind. Men waited in little boats to destroy them. The men waited to see the power of their tensed muscles and feel the clock-hammering of their hearts as they tore through the wind in their boats, ladling the surface of the sea. They hankered after the sound of their own laughter when the turtles writhed and somersaulted in their desperate but vain struggles to escape, and seemed to beg for mercy. They were animated by the circuit which flashed from a point on the turtle's back through their pressurized brains and along the co-ordinated muscles back to the shelled dome where they had planted the harpoon. They would beam, and split the ocean air with raucous shouts for they had convinced themselves that they were men – virile and all-powerful. There was the dismal spec-tacle of a harmless creature worn out by the demands of survival and he, Man, had inflicted great suffering on her. His lungs stretched out and drank the sea air greedily.

It is good to be on the sea. Mind you, one kills to provide food for one's family or to protect oneself against less scrupulous beasts. But the sight of blood is good; clean and refreshing like the rainbow – there's no denying that. It takes you back to where you began. So why not kill just for the hell of it? The earth's over-crowded with all manner of creatures – as the clergyman said, and he should know. The only trouble is that it is all over so quickly if you aren't very careful; alive one minute and dead the next. How to prolong this process needs brains. Maybe through it we might even come to understand this death phenomenon older than life itself. Let's make them suffer. Let's take them slowly across the barrier. But what has death to do with suffering? Both are natural laws – indisputable. Turn the creatures inside out and find what makes them go. But mind you don't get too close; some of these impudent creatures hit back. Find yourself a weapon; that's it – now you're more than a man; a hell of a man. No need for powerful muscles and large hearts. Leave that to the animals. Just a tiny speck of brain and a weapon will do. With that combination you could subjugate the whole world and crown the weapon Miss Universe.

Killing was no longer the mere law of survival nor a tribal ritual nor the flowering of the male into maturity over the limp shoulders of a slain lion. It was a hell of a sport earmarked for the crimson-eyed millionaires who would flock into a future Africa of devastating potential, and who had no further needs in life.

*　　*　　*　　*

A tired Dr Kawa sat beside Mr Marshall on the crossed plank of a large fishing canoe, facing the two paddle-men. In the bow, Sori crouched like a compressed spring.

He was massively built and his square face was covered on all four sides by greying curls of hair. The necks of his teeth were ringed with red through chewing cola nuts.

It was five o'clock in the morning and pitch dark. The stars blinked with fatigue after their long night's watch, and only the strained squeaks of the bats gave any indication of life in the undulating darkness of the land against a clear sky.

The waves lashed the shore gently and the men paddled easily, humming as they plunged, drove, twisted and withdrew the spoon-shaped blades of their paddles. It was too dark for Dr Kawa to see more than the moving outlines of their bodies but the soiled heavy smell of their sweat lingered in his nostrils. The boat rode smoothly, now rising on the crest of a wave now falling into the waiting hands of the parted water with a lapping noise. Occasionally the hooting of an owl seered the still coolness of the morning and its hollow echo rang loud from the hills; and each time this happened the tunings of an invisible orchestra rose from the depths of the land shadows as ducks, sparrows and the black and scarlet chinchiu voiced a somnolent ssh . . .

Dr Kawa put his hand to his mouth to stifle a yawn and asked casually, as if he did not expect a reply, when Mr Marshall had taken up the sport.

'Only a couple of years,' Mr Marshall replied with the carelessness of a mind not yet released from sleep. 'Since things got bad at home. It gives me an outlet, you know,' he said. Then suddenly becoming excited he added, 'Besides, it's a good justification for being out in this early stillness. It's all to do with birth – to see a new day being born.'

'I've been participating in the creative process myself

since I saw you at one o'clock,' Dr Kawa replied with a yawn.

'I'm sorry. You must be tired. But wait till the fun starts. You'll forget all about sleep. You can ask Sori; he's an old hand,' Mr Marshall said slapping Dr Kawa's knee affectionately. Dr Kawa turned towards the huge black shape crouching several feet away but could only see the white blades of Sori's teeth with their red necklaces hanging out of the darkness.

'Wait to see; you throw the spear so. Hai!' Sori screamed crashing one fist against the palm of the other hand. His voice seemed to spiral up from his groin. Again the land chorus cackled in protest.

'Just to see Sori in action is worth the trip,' Mr Marshall said almost at the top of his voice. Then feeling suddenly embarrassed by his unprovoked excitement he trailed his hand in the water.

'Massa; dat no safe,' Sori shouted leaping forward and flicking the dangling hand out of the water.

'Plenty shark in dis water, no safe,' he insisted by way of apologizing for his prompt if ungentle action.

Gradually they emerged out of the darkness and the vague shapes, as they followed the serrated coastline. First the shapes became more clearly defined in outline, then swelled into the third dimension of trees and shrubs. Then they were no longer still and the movements revealed the changing texture of their light-juggling surfaces. Suddenly the transformation was complete – the mist had faded, the yellow pigment of the eye bleached, and they were enveloped by the lilac translucence of dawn. Somewhere on the shining arc of the horizon a bright spot of light searched the surface of the water while nearer at hand the sleepy vegetation became restless with life, and each time a twig snapped a canopy of fluttering wings rose high ballooning in the wind, hovered, then moved forward and disappeared again into the greenery with loud rebellious cries. And from time to time the slithering bodies of the swordfish leapt shoulder high around the boat and, having scanned the intruders with inquisitive eyes, lop-lopped away to demolish some mullet which gave the water a ground-glass appearance not two hundred yards away.

With the shadows changing into real objects Sori turned round and watched for any moving objects which might be turtles; but as far as he could see there were none. As they crossed the mouths to the many inlets the boat would slow down so that he could comb the beaches for stragglers. But if there had been any on the beaches or just making their way out to sea, Sori would have waited till the turtle was well out to sea and riding the waves before giving chase. Killing turtles before they had been further exhausted by a chase was too tame a business.

The boat coasted in shallow water where a float of jelly-fish further softened its surface.

Mr Marshall sat tensed with expectation and ground his teeth. Involuntarily his knees snapped together and were held in a violent spasm. The possibility of an abortive venture tortured him. 'Where are the turtles?' he thought. 'Once the sun gets too hot and the sea rougher the turtles seek shelter. In any case harpooning in broad daylight takes half the fun away – it's like making love on the dining-room table.' Cautious drops of sweat began to pock-mark his face.

'We don't seem to be in luck with the brutes today,' he said rubbing his fingers with agitation as if to remove a stain.

'Actually it is a bit late in the season. They only come to lay their eggs and off they go again,' he added.

'Where do they go?' Dr Kawa asked hoping to keep himself awake by talking.

'God knows! They're a bit like vultures – homeless!' The thought again seemed to make him nervous and he rubbed his fingers together with slow milking movements. Then he became self-conscious about it and the more he struggled to stop himself the more obsessively violent the writhing movements became.

'I must talk. I must say something,' he thought but he had nothing to say. All were becoming disappointed. They had been out an hour and there were still no signs of a turtle.

'Not a single one. I tink we go back boss? Try again tomorrow maybe?' Sori suggested to break the silence.

Mr Marshall bit his lower lip and pulled his nose nervously. Through the corner of his eye he was aware of and resented the vague indifference on Dr Kawa's face; the face of a man who was less concerned with physical thrills than with the ideas behind them – the deep humanity which harmonized them and made them beautiful.

'We'll go as far as the next cove, shall we? What do you think? Maybe there's one over there eh?' he said to Dr Kawa; and added with quivering lips and despairing resolution, 'Then we'll turn back.'

Dr Kawa tried to calm him.

'There'll be others; tomorrow, as Sori says, if not today.'

The boat moved on. A broad shaft of light had now fanned itself over the sea but there were no turtles in sight. Suddenly Mr Marshall rose to his feet and stood in the middle of the boat with his arms akimbo facing the dense crowds of mangrove, reeds and sentry palms. The blanco from his plimsolls dissolved in the few inches of water which lay cradled at the bottom of the boat. Dr Kawa and Sori looked on in astonishment.

'Why don't you come? Cowards! Cowards!' he shouted waving his fists threateningly at the unheeding greenness, and leaning precariously backwards, with face tilted upwards, he projected his cries towards the sky. Sori leapt at him and held him firmly from behind. Mr Marshall continued to shout and struggle to free himself, but Sori's fine mahogany muscles slid this way and that like serpents as he swayed about to compensate for the violence of Mr Marshall and to prevent the boat from capsizing.

'H'all right boss! We catch one soon!' he kept repeating.

'Cowards! Cowards!' Mr Marshall shouted.

Dr Kawa held on desperately to the sides of the boat, which was now tossing dangerously, not daring to move.

The two paddle-men dropped their humming as well as their paddles, and preferring the devil of the sea which they knew, to the stranger of insanity, prepared to scuttle. Meanwhile the boat lurched and strained as it drifted towards the mangroves. Giving up the struggle at last Mr Marshall burst into a flood of childish weeping and further endangering the stability of the boat swung round and embraced a perplexed Sori who went on repeating, 'H'all right boss, we catch one ride'way.'

Dr Kawa was completely unnerved and felt weak in the stomach; the more so because of his own inadequacy to comfort Mr Marshall. He longed to be able to do something at that moment, to pour out strengthening words to his friend, yet he could not. He thought with dismay that the objective approach with which his medical training had equipped him had replaced his capacity to enter fully into the moods and sufferings of others. Further, his experience with Laura had numbed his powers to respond and it would be some time before he would be able sufficiently to dissociate himself and put them to good use for others. Even with Laura when the shock came he had felt impotent to grapple with it, to resolve it. He had withdrawn and it had seemed to him an action of grave despair. All the things he thought of saying or doing seemed to him like offering a blind man a lump of ice when he was expecting to be led across the road. He was gnawed with bitterness that the icy shield of protective aloofness, which he had cultivated during his lonely years in England when he had felt only a superficial friendliness tolerantly accorded him, had now stained his personality under the guise of good breeding. He remembered the searching look in his mother's eyes on that warm day of his arrival which had seemed to say; 'What have they done to you my boy?' He suddenly understood its meaning. He could do his duty; he was a good doctor – that was easy enough. But when it came to moral alliance he felt like a run-down dynamo. He had not forgotten his first meeting with Mr Marshall and the anguish he had felt at his own silence throughout their conversation. True, one had to draw the line with one's patients, but with a friend . . . with a friend one needed an identity of spirit. The whole human race was crying out for more identification of spirit.

'I only wanted a little flipper for Sonia,' Mr Marshall whispered. His face was buried in his hands and his shoulders were shaking.

'Not even a whole turtle; just a little flipper for Sonia.' Suddenly he stopped sobbing as if by clockwork and looked at his fleshy hands which shook with a coarse tremor. A self-pitying look spread under the metallic vagueness of his face as he showed them to Dr Kawa.

'Look! My hands are shaking, Kawa. I tell you they are shaking!'

'It's only the cold and the excitement.'

'But how can I catch a little flipper for Sonia with my hands shaking like this?'

'Big Sori can do it all by himself. We can just sit and watch,' Dr Kawa said.

'Oh no – we can't miss the excitement! Can we Sori?'

'No boss; big chase velly soon.'

The boat lurched forward with the full strokes of the paddle-men in whom fear had sowed new energy. They worked briskly and in silence not wishing to draw attention to themselves, but without staring at Mr Marshall they noticed every movement of his muscles and every change in the expression of his face.

'You know, Kawa!' Mr Marshall began, his eyes gleaming and his voice almost cracking with animation. 'Shark fishing may be tough but turtle fishing is much more exciting because it's drawn out. These creatures are dogged. They can't fight back – they can only run away – but they won't give in. Sometimes they surprise even me. You can "plunk" ten thousand thunderbolts through their backs and you think you've smashed all the furniture inside, yet they keep going. Sometimes I wonder what keeps them going.' Saying this he noticed his trembling hands and became tearful again.

'You know my wife hasn't been back for a whole week. I am terrified. By God I am terrified this may be the end,' he said.

'If she was going for good she'd be braz . . .' Dr Kawa began and hesitated to substitute another word.

'You think she'd be brazen enough? You think she would definitely say she was leaving me? Do you?' Mr Marshall asked.

'There's nothing false or dishonest about your wife,' Dr Kawa said thoughtfully. 'Not a virtue everyone can boast about.'

'Virtue!' Mr Marshall repeated, almost with conceit. 'She loves to torture me. She knows that every day she's away is a day subtracted from my life, so she'll pull out my life – stretch it out like syrup but won't break it.' He drew his finger-tips slowly apart to show how his wife had contrived to make his sufferings tenuous.

'Ah! But she doesn't realize she's dealing with a turtle. You'll never break; so cheer up,' Dr Kawa said tapping him on the shoulder and feeling pleased with the thought. It did cheer Mr Marshall up.

'Come on, let's make that next cove,' he said. 'There's a large turtle waiting there.'

Behind them Sori had been arranging and testing the tackle; poles, lines and heavy lead prongs and wooden clubs. When he was satisfied that the poles were not cracked and the lines were almost new and well secured round the little ring at the base of the flame-shaped prongs, Sori turned his attention once more towards the sea. Shielding his eyes from the quicksilver glitter of the water in the distance he scanned the surface with instinctive thoroughness. Ignorant of the background of Mr Marshall's domestic life, his attack of hysteria had struck Sori as a reaction to intense disappointment over the fishing, for which Sori felt partly responsible and longed to make reparation. Sori was murmuring a fisherman's prayer under his breath, inserting 'turtle' for 'fish'.

> God of the sea and land
> Keeper of turtle bands,
> Bring one with me face to face
> A turtle large and slow
> So I can sacrifice it in my place.

He reeled out the lines over and over, unwittingly changing their order and mixing up the rhymes in the concentration of his watch, and soon he had knitted the words into a little tune.

Meanwhile they reached the cove where Mr Marshall had agreed they would turn back, and the boat slowed down as usual. It was a small cove with the mangroves forming a bottleneck of an entrance. The beach was too steep for turtles to clamber up it, and the sand was spun into reticules as the tide and wind had left it.

A disappointed Sori suggested that perhaps they would find one on their way home.

'All right; turn back,' Mr Marshall said.

The paddle-men who were anticipating the order were already wheeling the bow in a wide circle. Their eyes gleamed and darted to the rhythms which crowded their brains. Suddenly Sori held his breath and pointed along the water's edge.

'Boss! Boss!' he screamed. 'Dere is one hell of a big one!'

Describing cones in the air with his arm, Sori tried to swing the boat back on course with the weight of his body. Not very far ahead the men could see something which looked like an upturned boat moving very slowly away from them. For some moments Mr Marshall sat like a stunned man, then cherubic wings seemed to appear at the angles of his mouth in a smile.

'Take it easy,' he said to the paddle-men, taking control of the situation. 'You see it's keeping close to the mangroves. If we chase now it might easily disappear into them. We've got to bide our time until she turns towards the open sea; then . . .'

The paddle-men accordingly rested their paddles, spat

into their palms and rubbed them vigorously together in readiness for the chase.

The boat slid easily forward. Dr Kawa felt the power of excitement created by the others enveloping him. Now that his desires were in sight of being fulfilled, Mr Marshall sat calmly with relaxed shoulders.

Sori made a final check of the tackle, testing the bamboo poles across his knee and wrapping a layer of newspaper round their bevelled ends so that they fitted more snugly into the harpoon ends. He tried the points of the prongs for sharpness against his thumb, attempted to break the knots which anchored the lines to the leaden ends and finally examined the entire length of the lines and arranged them in loose coils. Satisfied with everything he turned round to Mr Marshall with a deep laugh.

'All ready, boss,' he said.

'How many rods?' Mr Marshall shouted against the wind.

'Fifteen we got. Plenty enough.'

They were gaining on the turtle slowly.

They waited in suspense as the turtle reached a point beyond which they could not see. Would it turn in towards the land or out to sea, they wondered. For a whole infinite minute it disappeared and paddles dipped more energetically. Then it reappeared, its head vaguely discernible. It was making out to sea.

Sori allowed himself one wild shriek of delight and urged the men on. They re-applied the lubricant to their hands and the boat plunged forward. Now that it was cutting its way through the waves it pitched more fiercely, vibrated for an instant on the crest of a tearing wave, and lurched as it sprang forward into the waiting trough.

A wind rose, striking them sideways, and a velvet sun

hung perilously half-way to the vertical. A flight of squeaking gulls careered across the sky and melted away into distant clouds.

Mr Marshall's nostrils snorted loudly and the salt sprays made him even thirstier – the castled clown swam on in calm confidence.

'It can't have seen us,' Dr Kawa thought as he stole moist glances at the turtle bobbing up and down as it struggled obliquely through the waves.

'How could it, with so large a burden intervening? It's shell may have been a protection in the stone age; but not now.' He tried to reconcile his thoughts, which were in sympathy with the turtle, with the physical excitement which drove him on with the others.

And if she did. If she did see them bearing down on her, what could possibly save her now! No attitudes of terror could waive their sadistic appetites. Not even if she rolled over like a circus bear and offered her softer belly in a plea for mercy. No! It's too grotesque a misunderstanding, the thought of a simpleton. What is the object of hunting down a defenceless creature in so barbarous a fashion? Marshall says that it's to hear the clatter of broken glass as the leaden cloves pierce the shell again and again. To expiate the frustration of man against himself and against the universe. Yes, the sound – that's the thrill. A whole moment of auditory ecstasy.

'We'll take her on the left side,' Mr Marshall explained as he forced his left hand into a glove. 'Being left-handed I can plant some "fire tongues" just behind the neck so that they angle forwards. You get a better grip that way because with the brute trying to get away the prongs slip out sometimes. You get the idea? It's like nailing pegs round a race track.'

'What's the glove for?' Dr Kawa asked.

'This? I use a glove because the rings round the bamboo pole sometimes catch you between the fingers.'

They were quite close now, taking a deep curve on the port side of the turtle. Although it had apparently not seen them the vibrations must have reached it, for it swung suddenly to the right, adding a small reserve of speed. This movement brought the canoe in sight and the turtle corrected its direction by a compensatory swing to the half left position. It was heading towards the golden road which the sun had floated on the water. The pursuers gained ground and were shipped into a state of near frenzy.

Mr Marshall had moved to the fore part of the craft and leant Neptune-like on one of the poles. The coil of white line lay neatly on the cross-beam to which its other end was secured. Sori stood prepared to rearm Mr Marshall with poles and to retrieve those which would fly off the turtle's back like porcupine quills as the prongs penetrated deeper. With experience it was possible to thrust so skilfully that one could predetermine where the pole would come to rest – like leaving oneself another shot at billiards.

Dr Kawa sitting quietly in the middle of his plank felt the saliva from Sori's mouth on the back of his neck every time the latter shouted with delight at the meagre escape tactics of the turtle.

A wave lifted the bow high in the air and dropped it into a trough just behind the turtle; but at the moment when it seemed about to ride on the turtle's back it veered to the left and was alongside. Dr Kawa could see the clumsy hind legs flapping energetically as the turtle made desperate turns to escape. Mr Marshall took aim and blinded by a sudden rush of blood to his head thrust the lead into the shell farther behind the neck line than he had intended, with a profound groan of satisfaction. The turtle faltered and sat on its unsupported haunches under the weight of the thrust. It opened its mouth involuntarily as if to squeak with pain, but not a sound came out of it. It swam to the right with those muscles which were not paralysed by the blow, tilted like a badly holed ship. It swung round and made for the shore with the boat still veering in the opposite direction. The line spun out with a high-pitched whistle and became taut, turning the turtle a full backward somersault – a crimson flare flanked the line.

The boat swung round and rolled swiftly to head it off from the shore. The paddle-men, forgetting their recent fears, shrieked with pleasure, their arms and bodies dripping with sweat as the waves handed the boat on from crest to crest.

Once again the turtle was making for the open sea swimming on threes as a result of the disrupted equilibrium, half exposing the white shield between the scampering legs. Its strength was failing and the exhaustion of pain submerging all efforts to escape. The large flippers ploughed the water with wild coarse vengeance now, but still the rumple-necked centurion jerked cumbrously on with its comical hind legs, blood streaming in ribbons. But being in sight of the end was not the end, so on it struggled.

Dr Kawa felt the wounding thrust of eternal suffering from its soft eyes. He had never seen such sadness in black and white: not from the eyes of all the people he had seen dying had he seen engraved so bleak a vision of the grave; and his heart was momentarily arrested by the timelessness of the expression in them. He watched the toothless jaws open and shut at the end of a voiceless throat, yet there was no anger or reproach in the black tenements of the eyes. The unquenching fire of life still burned in them and forced the creature on with regardless dignity.

The excitement of the men had reached fever pitch and every spurt of blood was hailed with screams of delight. But while the others were thrilled by the sounds of the yielding shell, Dr Kawa felt a tightening in his stomach as if the blows had been aimed at himself.

The turtle was making instinctively for the stretch of sunlight which divided the waters in the distance when Sori plunged a cone so deeply that the lower end of the pole was also buried. The turtle subsided and with the sound of an airgun release, a volley of about forty ping-pong balls in their reddish-blue translucence – plop – plop – plop – floated to the surface of the water. This final giving seemed to overcome it. But Mr Marshall intoxicated by the colourful spectacle plunged a fatal cone across the base of its neck. The turtle made a forward dive, rolling over at the same time as if to offer its hind leg in a handshake, and became motionless.

'Now we must get her aboard without capsizing the boat,' Mr Marshall said.

'Why don't you trail her?' Dr Kawa asked, thinking it was ironical to pay the turtle the honour of a lift home.

'One word; sharks! We don't want to be trailed by them as well,' Mr Marshall said.

The turtle was soon roped and got aboard.

'What about dose heggs boss?' Sori asked pointing at the row of spheres drifting towards the shore.

'My Misses velly pleased wid some heggs.'

But Mr Marshall had had enough. 'No, no . . . we won't bother with them,' he said absentmindedly.

The boat drifted. Sori stared longingly after the eggs on their way to the mangrove bushes.

Perhaps there were birds or snakes which ate turtle eggs. What a waste.

They were on their way home, exhausted, a little gloomy.

'Better than I expected. I've never seen them lay eggs like that, never,' Mr Marshall said. The animation had gone out of his voice, limp and vapid like the organs after love-making.

'Did you get the thrill?' he asked Dr Kawa.

'It's impossible not to share your excitement,' he replied.

'Of course it's not always as easy as that. I've seen them turn a boat clean over. But you know what fascinates me is this business of mind over matter. You can watch the body, strong and determined gradually yielding to the superior force of death. But did you notice the eyes? I should have told you to watch the eyes.'

'As a matter of fact I did,' Dr Kawa said.

'That's the saving grace because you don't destroy the eyes. You can't. Look at her now. She's dead except for those eyes. They are challenging. When you first look into them they seem to say . . . "Well, I have seen all kinds of suffering which you know nothing about. See if you can show me any new kind of suffering. Prove yourself." Maybe that's why one does it . . . sets out to grind them. But do you know? I've never heard one cry out. I suppose they must have some kind of voice.' Mr Marshall was pulling his nose again with urgent downward movements and his voice was an uneven staccato which conveyed an unintended light-heartedness.

'What happens to it now?' Dr Kawa asked to distract him.

'When we get back Sori will distribute the meat to the villagers. They say it's tasty – a bit rubbery – but I've never tried it. Sori plugs the holes in the shell so well that you can't see where they were. They make good wash-tubs. I'd like you to have the breast-plate. Sori will look after it for you.'

'Thanks,' said Dr Kawa laughing. 'But what do you get out of it; nothing?'

'I collect the eyes. I've got a glass tank filled with preservative and I stick the eyes on a slate slab. I suppose I've got what? Say twenty pairs now?' Then he seemed to become depressed. 'They're all the same,' he added.

'Then why collect so many?'

'One day I hope to find a pair that's different. A green pair perhaps; a smiling pair of emeralds; a happy pair of turtle's eyes.'

'Curious thing, this suffering,' Dr Kawa said.

'How do you mean? One inflicts suffering to get rid of one's own, I suppose.'

'Quite!' Dr Kawa said. 'Isn't that the ultimate tragedy? That every moment of happiness necessitates a spun-out spiral of misery?'

They were making good speed homewards escorted by a school of porpoises. Sori was already mentally dissecting the turtle. Over the years he had worked out the quickest way to dissect a turtle which was also economical of the meat.

'Soon get dose eyes clean out for you, boss,' Sori shouted.

'Those flippers are too large for Sonia,' Mr Marshall repeated to himself. The boat ran aground on the beach.

'You will come home with me. Come and have some coffee. I don't like going into that house alone,' he said to Dr Kawa as they jumped down on to the wet sand.

'But of course I'll come in for a bit.'

'Mind you, I don't want to make you late for work, but I would be very grateful if you would.'

Sori said a brief good-bye promising to have the eyes ready by the morning and turned his attention to the catch. The two men walked slowly up the beach and along a path which meandered between tall rushes and so on to a road which served a row of houses. Skirting the Roman Catholic cemetery they crossed a field and beyond a hedge was Mr Marshall's property. They went in through the little gate and over the dried turf under the fruit trees towards the house.

The house was still asleep.

'Sonia won't be up yet,' Mr Marshall whispered as he led the way across the hall and up the balustraded staircase covered by a red carpet. When they were half-way up, Annie the cook came hobbling from the kitchen to see who was going upstairs.

'S'hat you?' she called with a husky voice.

'Hello Annie. The child not up yet, I suppose.'

'No. Mornin' Doctor,' Annie murmured, playing for time, as she struggled up the stairs after them. 'Had a good catch dis mornin'?'

'What's the matter Annie? I've never seen you climbing these stairs so quickly,' Mr Marshall said. Annie did not reply until she was quite close to them and then whispered with tears of happiness in her eyes, 'Misses back. Back not quite one hour ago,' she said. 'Misses don cam back – Misses home!' Annie repeated with emphasis.

'Where is she?' he asked in a matter-of-fact voice.

'Up in her bedroom. Don know whedder she's sleeping or not.' Mr Marshall squeezed Dr Kawa's shoulder and continued to climb the stairs.

'I say, I think I'll leave now. I'm sure everything will be

all right,' Dr Kawa said, anxious to avoid meeting Mrs Marshall.

'No! No! Come and have some coffee,' Mr Marshall insisted and hurried down a few stairs to stop Dr Kawa leaving.

'Please stay.'

'I bring some coffee in the sittin'-room right 'way,' Annie said lifting her voluminous skirt as she went downstairs.

On the landing they stopped opposite Sonia's door. Mr Marshall listened and then opened it as quietly as he could. Through the door Dr Kawa could see the sunlight streaming through the window and catching a rocking-horse squarely on the jaw.

'Is that you, Dr Kawa?' he heard Sonia say.

'It's Daddy. I didn't want to wake you,' Mr Marshall said.

'Where is Mummy?' she asked, still half asleep.

'She's in her room, Sonia.'

'Really?'

'Really,' Mr Marshall said; but Sonia had already pulled the blind over her consciousness and sighed back to sleep. Mr Marshall joined Dr Kawa on the landing and shut the door noiselessly behind him.

They went through an open doorway hung with a red velvet curtain into a large sitting-room. There were brass hangings on the walls between the family portraits. The floor was carpeted and an electric fan swayed from the ceiling. The flowers in the pots had not been changed for several days. Apart from a pile of women's magazines in one corner there was no other reading material about. The sitting-room led through a french window on to a large sun-terrace. The two men sat in silence while Annie served the coffee and left. Mr Marshall looked calm again.

'Would you like to see my collection?' he asked suddenly.

'Painting? I did not know you—' Dr Kawa began with enthusiasm but was interrupted.

'No; not that. My collection of eyes, I mean.'

'Perhaps another time – I really should be getting along.'

'Busy day ahead of you?'

'It's always busy,' Dr Kawa said getting up and emptying his cup. 'It doesn't seem to matter how early you start. There's always some work left over when you think you've finished.' He put his cup down on the table and was making for the door when Mr Marshall caught and stopped him.

'I say . . . I . . . Don't know how to say this . . . I . . . I'm very sorry about this morning. About my breaking down like that. I don't know what came over me,' he stammered.

'Good heavens! You forget it can happen to anybody. Now look at it this way. When a bladder fills beyond a certain point it empties itself. Similarly when the emotions get over-compressed they have to break through. The only difference is that they have more than one emergency exit.' Dr Kawa felt pleased with his analogy and thought it had the proper touch.

'Please . . . be honest with me,' Mr Marshall persisted, running his fingers nervously over Dr Kawa's shoulder. 'You . . . you don't think I'm going off my head or anything like that?'

'What gave you that absurd idea? You want me to be honest? Well here we are; you've set yourself a pretty high goal and to reach it you must strain every nerve and every willing cell in your body. But flesh and blood isn't steel and needs to shed its weight from time to time. You'd be in graver danger of going mad if you didn't give in completely now and again.'

'You're very kind to me. You're a true friend,' Mr Marshall said. 'But you know I sometimes wonder. One has no standards here; when one is dealing with the mind. It's . . . it's not like having a temperature; one can record that. One can't measure an idea, even less the effects of an idea. You can only hang on to it day after day, then all of a sudden you begin to doubt. One doubt goes round and round inside your head and collects more doubts. Next you begin to weaken; to be less sure of your idea; then the dreadful fear – fear of being wrong – of defeat. Fear of loneliness? I don't know. Fear of going mad.' He looked up at Dr Kawa and shook his clenched fists demonstratively. 'That's terrible! Terrible! I couldn't stand that. I couldn't stand the humiliation of going mad.' He knelt in an attitude of prayer on a tea stool and Dr Kawa saw the fear in his eyes and hurried to lift him by the elbow.

'But to doubt is healthy. It means that you have reserves; that you have elasticity. I have severe doubts myself. Everybody has.'

'Thanks again, Kawa. You've made me feel a lot better already.'

'I believe doubt is strength,' Dr Kawa added to seal his argument.

'But how it can paralyse you. How!' Mr Marshall gasped.

'Doubt only paralyses a fanatic; and at that stage it's already pathological.'

'Very thin ice eh, as the bishop said.' Mr Marshall forced himself to smile.

'Every new idea, every original or creative conception presents itself to our minds as a pathological focus and that's why we resist every novelty so strenuously. Resistance is a form of protection. In your case though . . .'

'Look, come and sit down a moment. This is getting interesting. Have some more coffee,' Mr Marshall interrupted showing Dr Kawa to a chair.

'No! I really must go. I shouldn't have started an argument. We'll talk about it some other time.'

'Come again soon. How about tonight?'

'You know how it is; depends on work.'

'I understand; but try.'

Dr Kawa turned to go and came face to face with Mrs Marshall. She was standing between the velvet folds of the curtain with her thick black hair hanging loose on her shoulders. Dr Kawa felt his heart contract at the sight of her and for an instant he thought it was due to anger. 'She is beautiful,' he admitted to himself reluctantly. 'There is a strong woman under that languid exterior.'

He felt strangely exposed under her heavy, direct glance and all the months during which he had studiously avoided their eventual contact appeared wasted, and the efforts puerile. Her eyes drew attention to themselves and Dr Kawa discovered something of the quality of the turtle's in them. Shifting, his eyes lingered round the breathing pores at the foothills of her breasts and stoel over the pastoral of her body.

'Good morning. I was just going,' he said, holding the curtain for her to come through. She did not move for a moment and then turned her face to him with a deliberateness that was almost challenging. Dr Kawa thought he saw the pulsations of her breasts and with each excursion a flood of perfume rose to his nostrils. He was further surprised when she spoke that there was a soft correctness in her manner and that there was none of the caressing seductiveness he had expected to find.

'Dr Kawa?' she said at last offering a limp hand.

Mr Marshall had not heard her come in and was unlocking the french windows. He swung round and rushed towards them leaving the window half open. His manner expressed a passionate admixture of pleasure, confusion and embarrassment at seeing his wife. He had always hoped for a meeting between his wife and Dr Kawa since he still longed to create a better impression in Dr Kawa's mind about her than he thought existed, and also because he felt convinced that Dr Kawa's influence for good would prevail over her. All these subjective and projected motives made him act unnaturally.

'This is my wife, Kawa,' he said, rubbing his hands together awkwardly after they had already squeezed hands.

'Call me Clara,' she said quietly as she eased herself into a low arm-chair.

'You must forgive her being in a dressing-gown, but it's early; isn't it? It's oh . . . I'd say . . .' Mr Marshall began.

'If you'll excuse me, I was just leaving,' Dr Kawa said, inclining his head.

'Please!' she said, pointing her polished nails towards a chair. 'Please, I shouldn't make demands on your time I know, but won't you stay a little longer?' she asked and, sensing that Dr Kawa was determined to excuse himself, added with a faint suggestion of intimacy, 'So that I don't feel that you're leaving because of me.'

The appealing warmth of her voice and its disarming – almost commanding – charm irritated Dr Kawa.

'I would like to, but I must get to the hospital now, I'm afraid,' he said firmly.

'I am asking you a favour, Doctor,' she said stressing the last word; then turning to her husband added, 'You ask him Jackie, perhaps he will stay for you.'

Mr Marshall could not remember when his wife had last asked him for anything, and the implication that he could persuade Dr Kawa where she had failed overwhelmed him.

'Clara, you know how busy doctors are. Can't we let him off this once? He must get off to his patients you know,' he said.

But Dr Kawa was determined not to stay and with the minutes he felt an antagonism gain ground inside him. He had always tried to preserve an open mind towards Mrs Marshall, and while he could avoid a head-on involvement it had not been too difficult, but face to face with her he felt unable to place the unspoken guilt which was his as well as everybody else's verdict on her conduct. There was something insufferably forgivable in her although he did not know what it was.

'What trick is she up to now? Why should she think that she can confound all men? She can have her way with Methuselah, twirl him round her finger but not with me,' he said to himself. He bowed again and moved towards the door.

'Is one life more important than another?' she asked with disconcerting calm. Mr Marshall looked wildly from her to Dr Kawa and back at her, not understanding a word.

Dr Kawa raised his head on his bowed shoulders and for the first time looked her straight in the eyes. Even now there was not a trace of the glamour or seduction which he had expected to find and he felt somewhat deceived. He was looking at a woman starkly embellished yet possessing inner nobility, and she had asked him a question. He saw a whole world portrayed in the hot depths of her eyes. Such beauty – such soul stirring warmth – so magnificent a combustion of life energy, and such seemingly sadistic inhumanity. So much joy, pleasure and hope on the one hand and so ignoble a burden of pain and suffering on the other. What absurd logic! His thoughts pulled him irresistibly towards her and for the present they had obscured the question.

'Is it such a difficult question?' she prompted.

'No!' he answered recovering himself. 'The danger lies in giving too simple an answer.'

'But what is the point of the question?' her husband wanted to know. 'What is the point?'

'You said Dr Kawa had to rush off because of his patients,' she said.

'Yes?'

'And I asked whether one life was more important than another.'

'I know you did. But I don't see the point.'

Dr Kawa sat on the edge of the settee. He did not admit to himself that what attracted him about her had something to do with her eyes, her breasts, and her knees which lay exposed between the edges of her dressing-gown. Rather he told himself that he was fascinated by her spirit, by what she was going to say next; by her unpredictability.

'No; I don't think one life is more important than another as such, but the value of what one life achieves can be altogether out of proportion with another,' he said.

'As a doctor do you make decisions on the basis of the first or the second factor?' Once again Dr Kawa was impressed by the appeal of the unexpected. He would never have guessed that she would be as interesting to talk to as to watch.

'Fortunately I am never called upon to make the second

kind of assessment, though I can imagine situations where the question might arise.'

'I don't see the point of all this; and Clara, Dr Kawa wants to get to the hospital,' Mr Marshall protested.

'I haven't forgotten,' she said without shifting her eyes from Dr Kawa. 'Tell me Doctor, is there a cure for cancer?'

'Not – not *you*!' her husband whispered.

'What does it matter who?' she replied curtly, her lips hardening.

'It depends on so many factors. Site, rate of growth, the stage at which it is first discovered and so on.'

'What about a cancer at the back of the nose?'

'I don't know of a cure in the ordinary sense but there are methods of treatment which claim some success. As I said earlier, depending on the type and the stage of growth.'

'Can you cope with it here? In Freetown?' Clara asked.

'Since you are consulting me, don't you think you should tell me who the alleged patient is and so on?'

'I am sorry. I should have started from the beginning.' She shifted uncomfortably in her chair and Dr Kawa realized that she too was under strain.

'I have not been told the patient's name, let alone seen the patient, yet you present me with a diagnosis and expect my comments,' he protested mildly.

'Not very professional; I'm sorry. I'm not a very methodical person as Jackie will vouch. But I shall tell you everything when you have answered my question. Can you treat it here?'

'I certainly cannot, and I don't know that any of my colleagues has made a special study of the problem. I would say that the best hope would be to send the patient abroad.'

'To England?' she asked.

'If I am to recommend somewhere, yes.'

Clara lit a cigarette. Her fingers trembled smoothly.

'Now Mrs Marshall,' Dr Kawa said in his professional voice. 'If you don't require any more advice I'm afraid I must go.'

Mrs Marshall turned towards her husband with a forced smile. 'Jackie, you want to know who has cancer? Freddie.'

Mr Marshall leant forwards in his chair with his eyes wide open.

'Your boy-friend? Your boy-friend has cancer?' he asked. Then leaning back in his chair with head tossed back he began to laugh. What started as a giggle soon swelled into a loud paroxysm which he had no power to control. The loud satanic sarcasm of his laugh filled the house while the other two watched in silence. Then almost as suddenly as he had begun, Mr Marshall relapsed into gloom.

'I don't understand . . . everything seems crazy. Freddie? A strong healthy-looking boy dying of cancer?'

'We don't know that he is dying,' Dr Kawa suggested. Clara turned to him the same look of pity which she had levelled at her husband during his hysteria and nodded slowly.

'He is dying. He has been hiding it for five weeks. Then the pain got too much for him, and the bleeding from the nose became frequent. He went to see the specialist at the hospital who said straight off that nothing could be done. It had gone too far.'

'Did no one suspect it?' Dr Kawa asked.

'I did. I knew something was wrong but naturally I did not know what it was. I did not know it was the pain that made him so irritable. Also he was using rather a lot of perfume to drown the smell lately.'

'Did Mr Heinrich say how long?'

'A month if he's unlucky. He says it has spread to the neck.'

'Why unlucky?'

'Freddie can't bear the pain for another month. Not a whole month. It's something fearful when he runs out of injections,' Clara said. In spite of her intangible innocence, the fresh morning bloom of her face, the evening wrinkles were already apparent, and she looked frightened and alone.

Mr Marshall left the room muttering to himself, 'Freddie? It can't be true. My nephew; my own flesh and blood. My sister's boy.'

When he had gone Dr Kawa rose to leave.

'I can't tell you how sad it makes me to hear this, and I am only sorry that I can't be of more help,' he said.

Clara saw him out to the landing.

'I won't come down, but I shall need your help later on, and I want to thank you for loving Sonia.'

Annie was waiting in the hall downstairs.

'Don' like dee goin's on in dis 'ouse, Doctor. Enough to sen' de wrath of de good Lord down on us,' she said as he went out of the house.

Chapter Ten

Darkness falls where light has been. At the Marshalls' home the days lengthened and spun into coils with the marching strains of death. Freddie dwindled into the charred remnant of a tree after a bush fire, within the turning of the moon. His youthful arrogance crumpled into the defiance of old age, and the agile dare-devil glint of his eyes wilted under the greenish tint of accumulated secretions. He was no longer able to endure the exhaustion of a shave, and his beard hung like a rough carpet from the bony prominences of his cheeks, obscuring much of his face and making his head look larger than it was. The proud neck muscles had wasted away and the feeble stream of his pulse became exaggerated as it trickled between the glandular masses. He had taken on the transparency of approaching death.

Since everything had to be done for him, Clara's life had become one of complete service, and although he did not complain, every movement, even the effort of breathing, caused him pain. But his greatest tormentor was the heat: it made him sweat like a sieve and this meant a frequent change of clothing which caused him pain and exhausted him. His air passages were already partially blocked by the growth and the heat almost suffocated him. Yet when the electric fan was turned on the constant droning jarred his nerves so that he would become restless with the pain in his ears and he felt as if his eardrums would burst.

For several days the sky remained uncompromisingly clear as if the usual blustering October weather had been tucked away as old women do their purses. The heat was stifling and the mercury in the thermometer in Freddie's room looked as though it spurt toward the ceiling. Everyone, Clara most of all, prayed for rain or a gust of those October winds of desert coolness which were guaranteed to sweep away the mud tracks of September as well as the oppressive canopy of heat.

Clara spent silent hours and days in the plush arm-chair by his bed massaging the cold bones of his hand or whispering endless silver-papered protestations of love to him. In the blue light of the shaded lamps she had learnt to recognize the change in tempo of his breathing which told her that his pain was growing more severe, and she would sponge his paper-thin forehead with iced water, turning her face away as she gave him yet another injection of morphia. After each administration she would collapse into her chair, leaving the flies which swarmed round his open mouth to their own devices for a time. But the continuous vigil soon made inroads on the freshness of her eyes and the tight contours of her body slackened with loss of weight. Sometimes as the sun rose high in the sky and the acrid sweet smell of decay filled the room she would swallow quick successive mouthfuls of the thick air to suppress the rising nausea inside her; overcome at last she would rush out on to the sun terrace, to wring out her empty stomach over the geranium tubs.

Freddie's sleep became hesitant and twilit as if he were on guard against the arrival of death, but really because the increasing doses of morphine were less and less effective against the pain. Sometimes when Clara's arm tired of shifting the flies with her handkerchief and her heart became over-weighted by her new devotion, she would lean her head against his arm and fall asleep. Then when the effects of the previous injection had worn away she would wake suddenly to the agony of his groans and the restless billowing of his breathing, and with trembling hands she would plunge the needle into his flesh and squirt the bland fluid of relief. Sometimes she watched the effects of the injections and she could see the hard lines of pain begin to melt away almost at once, and a pleasurable relaxation spread over his face. This stimulated a new perception in her, and she felt a curious love for the fine parchment of his skin through which she thought she could see the irony of a smile.

'They are narrow margins – the beauty of life and the exquisite nobility of death. In that fragile nose bridge which would cave in under a child's fist, and that bold line of the forehead is so much vital energy. There must be, for how else would I continue to be bound so closely to him!'

They were arduous days for Dr Kawa, on whose slight shoulders had descended the duties of doctor and general factotum to the Marshall family; and he found himself making the domestic as well as the professional decisions. He and Clara had been flung together in an almost intense collaboration about which he scarcely had time to reflect. As usual he had not been able to make up his mind to take a positive stand; he had accepted his position calmly.

On the day that Freddie joined the Marshall household, Dr Kawa had returned home to find a letter from Clara waiting on his table. In it she had worded her appeal for help in more urgent terms, minced it with the voice of command and perfumed the result with her laying down of arms. Dr Kawa had gone over at once through the space in the hedge.

He was acutely disturbed by the awareness that he was driven by Clara's tenacious will-power and his own need to grapple with it, rather than by the needs of her expiring lover. He had gone in through the back door and was wiping his shoes on the mat, his mind preoccupied with the situation, when he noticed Mr Marshall reflected in a mirror which hung at the top of the stairs which led down to the cellar. But he had so much else to think about that he only noticed that Mr Marshall's jaws were moving and that his eyes conveyed approval. Dr Kawa wondered vaguely why he felt suddenly guilty at seeing Mr Marshall and was inclined to hurry away up the stairs when the thought struck him that down there in the cellar was Mr Marshall's little museum which he had been invited to visit but had not had time to do so. The thought so insinuated itself among all his more pressing concerns that he hesitated and looked at the mirror again. Suddenly he was filled with a horror and revulsion which he did not immediately understand. As he watched, Mr Marshall dipped his hand into a rectangular glass tank and picked out an object which he produced between his index finger and thumb. He dipped it into a bowl and examined it with a sad expression. Then he spun the object by rolling its stalk between his fingers and smelt it approvingly. He then put it to his mouth and plucking it like a cherry with his lips off its stem, chewed away with the same satisfied expression as before.

On hearing Dr Kawa's footsteps hurrying down the stairs Mr Marshall turned sharply. Recognizing Dr Kawa, he fished for something in the tank and held out an object with a truant grin on his face.

'Have one,' he said with the gentle persuasiveness of a

child offering a sweet to another he does not know very well.

Mr Marshall was eating his collection of turtles' eyes. Dr Kawa stood speechless.

'I want to talk to you,' he said, accepting the proffered eye and tossing it back into the formalin.

Mr Marshall's eyes grew vague. He looked into the tank and then reprovingly at Dr Kawa. As Dr Kawa led him by the arm towards the stairs he seemed to be straining himself to remember something. 'Me? You want to talk to me?' he asked innocently tapping his fingers on his chest.

'Yes, let's go upstairs. It won't take long,' Dr Kawa said firmly.

'Who are you?' Mr Marshall asked meekly, still staring at Dr Kawa. Then with a sudden aggressiveness he shouted; 'Who are you to come into my house and interrupt my lunch?' He freed himself from the other's grip and backed away from Dr Kawa with an anger tinged with terror. He stumbled against the tank, turned round and stared back at the row of eyes before him. His expression softened.

'I want to talk to you about Clara,' Dr Kawa said without moving. At the mention of his wife's name Mr Marshall ran forward and grabbed Dr Kawa by the arm, moving his grip up and down the length of it.

'Is something wrong?' he said with vapid intensity. 'Is something wrong with Clara?' he asked sobbing and laying his head on Dr Kawa's shoulder.

'No, nothing is wrong with Clara, and you've no need to upset yourself,' Dr Kawa said leading him up the stone steps.

'Then why can't I finish my lunch?'

In the hall Dr Kawa signalled retreat to an anxious

Annie who came bounding out of the kitchen when she heard the sobs. She obeyed, sulking because she felt her place as mother-figure and trusted servant usurped.

'Are you the undertaker?' Mr Marshall asked eyeing Dr Kawa suspiciously.

'No.'

'You're his assistant. You send him customers,' Mr Marshall said pointing at Dr Kawa as if with sudden recollection. Dr Kawa smiled and sighed with relief when they were safely in Mr Marshall's bedroom. There, he opened the windows and pulled back the curtains so that the light poured in, and the stagnant air began to unwind like a python.

'I shall send Annie with a drink and then I shall come and have one with you,' Dr Kawa said as he left him alone.

Mr Marshall sat in his favourite chair wallowing in the pleasure of a holy smile – he was thinking that he was a bishop.

*   *   *   *

Death attracts sightseers, flies and vultures alike; the visitors poured in to the Marshalls' home from all over Freetown. Some to see the inside of the much-discussed house, others in anticipation of a liberal celebration, and not a few who had joined the end of the queue out of habit. With nobody to look after them they sat on the landing and in the hall, some even making do with the stairs, and waited for a call to tears. Day after day they waited in their sombre dresses, their throats parched with the heat; and as Annie did not have the keys to the liquor cupboard, discontented murmurs spread among the potential mourners like an evil smell.

'This has never happened before. A funeral without a

single drop of whisky – even a little sherry to make us feel at home,' said a stout woman who had held the head of the queue for several hours and was not content with the reception.

'But he's not dead yet,' whispered another who was less certain why she was there.

'Supposin' he dies suddenly, where do they expect us to get the tears from if they don't warm us inside?' the first woman said, raising her voice.

'Is that what we supposed to do?' asked the other.

'Yes . . . s . .s . .' whispered the first sarcastically. 'Have you never been to a funeral before?' she asked.

'This is my first,' the smaller woman confessed.

'Ah! What have you been doing with your life?' said the first, rolling her eyes away disapprovingly.

A wave of nudges started in the hall and spread up the stairs but when it reached the woman who did not know what she was supposed to do she lifted her head with indignant surprise at the transmitter of the nudge.

'The doctor . . . that's the doctor,' she was told by an agitated woman who was anxious lest the information should not reach the top of the queue in time.

Dr Kawa who was making his third visit that day had to squeeze through the crowds. 'What pests,' he thought. 'Not a single one of them bears anything but scorn and hate for Clara and Freddie, yet they sit here all day for what they can get. What nauseating hypocrisy!'

'Okushe,' they moaned sullenly as he wended his way through them, and he heard the affected sighs of sympathy ring in the hall below.

'That must be the room,' someone said leaning forward and pointing with her eyes and eyebrows at the door through which Dr Kawa had just disappeared. At that moment a terrifying scream from Mr Marshall's bedroom shook the house to its foundations and the women looked at each other with mixed feelings.

'They say he's going off his head,' one woman said.

'Poor man. Who wouldn't,' said another.

'Ah, this is mean O! Not a drop. Not a single biscuit,' the first woman persisted, as she tried to make her head more comfortable on her stout shoulders. 'Worst of all I did not breakfast this morning. Poor people would never treat us like this.' Reluctant but furious she vacated her place on the landing and left the house, shaking the dust off her feet.

'Rich people! Hmmm!!' she said and spat on the hot gravel outside.

* * * *

During those difficult days Annie suffered the most, because she was not actively involved in what went on upstairs. A deep feeling of helpless devotion gnawed within. While one part of her yearned for the recovery of a family of which she felt herself a part, she sorrowed for herself on the other hand, for to be cut off from activity, mirrored in her mind the end of her usefulness and even of her days. She was to be seen waddling over the polished floor in the hall with her apron pulled up to her eyes weeping because the very best soup which she had made out of the very best cow's trotters could not be eaten by Freddie and would not be eaten by Mr Marshall, so she had been obliged to dilute it with her tears and pour it down the sink. This confession produced mixed feelings among the mourners, some of whom sympathized with her and prophesied that one day God would wake up to the cries of the down-trodden and needy, while others were indignant that she had thrown the soup away without offering it to them.

For three days Mr Marshall had locked himself in his bedroom in darkness refusing to see anyone, and this had stimulated the positive side of Annie's nature. At each visit she demanded from Dr Kawa that something be done. On the first day she demanded that Dr Kawa should break in the door. On the second, with axe in hand, she had threatened to use it herself if the doctor would not, and he had persuaded her that two days of solitude far from proving harmful would be beneficial to Mr Marshall. On the third day he had arrived just in time to save her from a certain fall as she attempted to climb a ladder of stacked cases so that she could look down on her master over the top of the wall from an adjoining room. Annie had burst into tears of shame because she had been caught in so foolish a pursuit and had gone to the kitchen blowing her nose noisily into her apron and beating her thighs with remorseful fists.

'A curse is on dis 'ouse,' she swore.

Later Dr Kawa enraged her by suggesting that she should lie down and rest. 'Rest? No rest for me till Master open dat door and drink some soup,' she had said, waving her chubby hands defiantly as she crawled downstairs backwards because it was safer and easier on her joints.

The houseboy who did not like the melancholy of the days had disappeared. It was left for Dr Kawa to implore the nuns at the convent to take Sonia over, as he did not think it proper to have the child in the house.

Three weeks later on a Friday morning a vast net darkened the sky spreading from the north-east like an eclipse. Before the windows of the houses could be shut it had alighted, clustered a foot deep on the ground and was gone in a matter of minutes. A multitude of locusts had stopped for a brief refuelling in their gluttonous flight, and when they left there was not a green thing to be seen for miles around. The trees stood tearful in their nakedness. People said it was an augury of doom.

In the wake of the locusts a crescent blackness loomed low in the southern sky and soon spread over the mountain ranges. Before it an advance guard of whirlwinds spun the dried leaves and raised the dust to the eyes as in a sand-storm. Legs were knotted in skirts as women hurried home and men jog-trotted after their trilbys. A silver line burnt its way through the blackness and soon the earth seemed to crack and the noise of its falling away skipped over the hills in a circle of echoes. Loose gates and windows were torn off the decapitated houses and stacked helter skelter; then followed the agonizing pelting down of the rain.

Clara woke from the chair where she had spent the night to the banging of the windows and the lashing of the curtains this way and that, filling the room with a rejuvenating freshness whose magic she had forgotten during the recent weather. Her first impulse was to run out into the storm; instead, with a smile on her face, she went to shut the doors and windows. It was a long time since she had smiled. Her breathing grew excited and her pores opened wide so that her skin itched. She pressed her nose hard against the window-pane and watched the wind toss and strain the trees, uprooting some and splitting others. She blinked and hid behind the curtain when the sudden flash of lightning pierced the clouds, and with clenched fists cowered in anticipation of the peal of thunder. The sound of the rain was that of a thousand drills being driven through the roof simultaneously, but muffled and soft; it filled her with a warm desire. Clara had always been frightened by storms because they made her feel helpless and insignificant by their sheer ruthless majesty; yet she loved them for the sense of purification which they seemed to bring to her and to everything around.

With sudden inspiration she moved back to Freddie's bedside with a joy heightened by its foreboding and covered his hand with hers. Kissing it tenderly she buried her face in the quilt of pale blue silk, rubbing her face passionately against it as she dropped his hand under her dress and folded her breasts round it. Every muscle in her body contracted in a slow protracted spasm shaking her from head to foot. She had momentarily forgotten the storm, and her heart no longer raced. Clara walked to the tall mirror framed in the door of the wardrobe in a corner of the room where Freddie could not see it. In the blue light she saw herself as a shadow, elusive and indeterminate, yet embodying a greater reality than the concrete Clara, because it was engraved with a terror and tenderness. Only when a flash of lightning brightened the room and she shied automatically did she notice the lines at her temples and the corners of her eyes, and she realized she was growing visibly older. The thought filled her with sudden panic and remorse and she fell on her knees in front of the mirror with devastating awareness of being alone. She felt as though she had thrown herself over a cliff edge and was hurtling down its craggy surface at death-speed; only she was conscious and knew what was happening and what to expect at the end of the fall. She gasped as if she had been dreaming and put her hand over her mouth to stop herself from screaming. She turned round suddenly, still on her knees, as if to make certain where she was, and recoiled again at the guttural sound of

Freddie's breathing. The eyes of the shadow in the mirror were full of fear.

Outside, the storm rolled on indifferently plundering the land, the lightning flashes growing more dazzling and terrifying. Clara longed for someone with whom she could share her fear; someone who would put his arms round her; just to feel the friendliness and security of a human embrace. She thought of Dr Kawa. Would he come? Would he wait until after the storm? Friends never seemed to be there when one needed them, she thought. Is Dr Kawa a friend? Would he come?

The room was now illuminated by a succession of flashes, Clara raised herself on her knees. The flashes seemed to link hands and falling on a naked wire on the wall chased round the room unable to escape. A sizzling noise flew round after them throwing off sparks and puffs of smoke. Insane with terror she sprang to her feet and rushed towards the door. Unable to find her way through the curtains she fastened herself to a firm object within the confusion of its folds. She was breathing loudly and quickly – a pair of arms clutched her shoulders and she pressed her trembling body crushingly against their owner. The curtain found its way round her and she knew she was in Dr Kawa's arms. Hardly knowing what she was doing she stood on her toes and moulded her lips on his, caressing all his opposites with her body.

When they had finally disengaged and Dr Kawa reached the bed, Freddie's eyes were closed but Dr Kawa knew he was not asleep. He was very weak but tried to open his eyes as Dr Kawa gave him his injection, a twisting smile wavering on his thin lips. Clara was still draped in the cool lines of the curtain as he had seen her on that morning of the turtle fishing. He reloaded the syringe and put it on the table, walked towards Clara and kissed her between the pillars of her breasts.

In the sitting-room it was Clara who broke the tense silence. 'How much longer?' she pleaded.

'I don't know; might go on for several days yet.'

'How is Jackie?' she asked. It was the first time she had asked about him and Dr Kawa saw a glimmer of tender affection under the callousness of her physical beauty.

'He isn't at all well. I'm afraid . . . I'm thinking . . .' he hesitated and considered whether it was time to be frank with her. Clara's eyes fixed on his, serene and reconciled.

'He'll have to go to the mental hospital,' he said hurriedly. 'It's the only thing to do, Clara.'

'He's mad!' she gasped pressing her hands between her knees and staring at the carpet as if to read an explanation from it. Dr Kawa slid forward in his chair with arm stretched out to touch her. He wanted desperately, painfully to comfort her.

'You must not think you are responsible for all the world's sins,' he said.

She got up and walked towards the french window. Stood there watching the blue sky now dotted with clouds and still wet with the rain dripping off the trees. The chickens had come out into the sun to dust their wings.

Next door Freddie had made a final effort to reach the syringe on the table and had conveyed himself peacefully into the unknown.

*   *   *   *

The funeral took place the following day, hastily arranged because corpses did not tolerate the heat. The Church which had refused to release Mr Marshall from his marriage vow also felt unable to give Freddie a Christian burial. A speedy disposal of the dead had replaced the native communion with illness and death in the past. While the plain coffin of brown wood, glass-fronted, was being shouldered down the stairs between columns of mourners, Freddie's bedroom was already being fumigated.

Freddie's death produced a further and sudden deterioration in Mr Marshall's condition. It was as if he had willed and desired all the suffering of the recent years of his life on himself, and with the disappearance of the instrument of his distress, no longer desired to face reality. For several days he had insisted on remaining in a darkened room; his chin was stubbled and his face haggard. But during the exhausting twenty-four hours before Freddie's death Dr Kawa had noticed a new dimension of unreality in Mr Marshall's eyes.

The cortège moved slowly. Clara in her black dress looked serene and beautiful to Dr Kawa, walking beside her with bowed head and hands clasped behind him. She was at her most lovable, and had gone beyond promise into fulfilment. Yet he had not accepted to himself the responsibility of loving her.

The wreathed hearse warbled along on rusty axles to the determined pull of six sombre and poker-faced men who evidently took their job seriously, yet gave the impression that they had no personal relationship with death; that they would have been surprised if they had been told that they also one day would be the subjects of such a procession. Black-suited with blue plimsolls on bare feet they showed a bewildering identity of character and appearance. Under their bowlers, they carried similar temperaments. But the harmony of their disposition did not extend to their opinions of each other; each thinking the others were so much dead weight, and but for himself alone the hearse would tumble into the ravine behind them. Thus their silences were broken and spiced with abuse.

'Pull the b-b-b-bloody r-r-rope h-hohohover,' stammered one of the number looking over his shoulder and lifting his feet high off the ground as though he was on stilts.

'Mind your damn business,' shouted another leaning forward with his bit of rope over his shoulder.

'Alleluya!' some of the mourners echoed.

'No r'spect for the dead!' another.

'What these Trade Unions are doing to us; it's because they know they are indispensable,' lamented a third.

The procession moved uphill along the sultry road halting or diverting the heavy Saturday traffic, but even the Arc roads were crowded with vehicles and some motorists after chasing round the detour, found they still had to wait when they got back to the main road.

'I am Alpha and Vinegar,' shouted an old man earnestly. He had assumed the place of a priest. A fat woman exploded in high-pitched laughter and retired to the kerb to control herself. A volley of squeaks shot through the crowd under the stern gaze of the hearse-puller in the black suit.

The old man oblivious of his error or that he was guilty of causing a commotion went on stamping his cane on the melting tar.

'I am the firs' and the never never,' he cried.

'Pa Randoll has been at the rum again,' a woman said.

'Ah! It's ole age, you know.'

''Is memory is goin'.'

Where they turned off the main road on to the red earth of the countryside with its wheel tracks, one of the hearse-men acted as traffic controller and, advancing with his face to the procession, signalled an elaborate right turn. The wheels squeaked and jangled as they rolled down the red path towards the cemetery. The diggers were laying down their spades and wiping the sweat off their necks when the procession arrived. The crowd arranged itself dutifully around the grave under the shade of a stout tree, and the coffin was laid in position on some planks set transversely over the grave with two lowering ropes ready.

Pa Randoll who was officiating removed his skull-cap and exposed a glistening scalp to the sun. Some among the crowd worked up a tear and held it poised in spite of their subdued giggles. Pa Randoll clasped his cap to his chest and lifted his face towards the sky, and began a prayer.

'When these two are joined together in Thy Tabernacle O God, may 'e rest in peace,' he intoned. But the stolen glances which swept round the grave were accompanied by a lusty 'Amen!'

Clara stood by the graveside on a pile of earth which was still wet, and watched the men lower the coffin. The planks were removed while the coffin was supported by ropes, then there was a sound of falling rubble as the ropes ran against the edge of the grave and ended with a thud as the coffin reached the bottom. The ropes were pulled out with a grating sound which set her teeth on edge.

A hymn was sung.

Clara moved towards the head of the grave where she could see Freddie's face through the glass facing. The delicate face with the plugged nostrils and the soft stubbled chin over a white bow tie seemed to change into the features of the Freddie she had known -- when he was handsome and gay and proud. Her chest began to heave and her eyes misted over with tears. Dr Kawa stood behind her with his eyes closed. A number of women wailed with their shawls over their eyes. Clara felt as though it was all a dream. She heard the old man say 'Dust to dust' and then the thud-thud of the wet earth falling on the coffin.

'Ashes to ashes,' the frail determined voice continued. Clara stopped to take a handful of earth burying her nails and fingers deep in its red wetness. She was close to the earth and could smell the dampness and decay. Tears poured freely from her eyes and she could not see clearly. She began to straighten herself; the soft earth under her feet began to move. A woman opposite shrieked and extended a helping hand across the far distance of the grave. Dr Kawa opened his eyes. Clara slid into the grave, her left foot smashing through the glass facing of the coffin with a blood-curdling shattering of glass. She did not move from the crouching position in which she was folded over her dead lover, and did not utter a sound.

Dr Kawa, astride the grave, took her by the armpits while someone who had leapt in after her and was standing on the coffin lifted her up to him.

Clara was unconscious when they finally got her out and laid her under a tree. The cuts round her ankle bled freely. Dr Kawa bound the ankle with borrowed handkerchiefs and tried to revive her with smelling salts. His hand shook slightly as he waved the bottle under her nose.

For a second after the incident Pa Randoll had remained glued to the ground with horror and incomprehension, his jaws stuck in the articulation of 'ashes'. He crossed himself several times with skinny fingers. Then his knees began to give way and he was moved away from the graveside just in time before he collapsed.

Fear flashed through the crowd.

When Clara sneezed and showed the first signs of a return to consciousness only the labourers shovelling back the earth as quickly as they could, and the birds remained. The sound of crunching bone as her foot had flattened the face of the corpse like a sand-castle haunted her, and she relapsed momentarily into unconsciousness.

Dr Kawa looked around and saw there was no one to help him. Even the gravediggers who threw sidelong glances at them hurriedly looked away when they saw the cry for help in his eyes.

Dr Kawa saw for the first time how nakedly friendless Clara was against the bravura of her living, and he felt even closer to her.

'No one can survive without human warmth, and no one should; whatever their guilt,' he thought.

Kneeling there under the sun's glare he thought how fortuitously everything had happened. His relationship with the Marshalls for instance; that had started with Jackie's tale of woe, and then the turtle had taken it on a stage further; and now! When he had begun his frequent visits as doctor and friend he had consoled himself with the thought that sooner or later it would all be over, and he would return to the relative peace of his practice, unscathed. But since the thunderstorm things had certainly changed for him. He did not yet think of it as love; no, that was too grotesque a commitment. But he had felt responsible for her, and now he felt she belonged to him.

The sun grew fiercer. Dr Kawa looked round at the graves, many of which had been flattened by the rain and with neglect. There was not a living soul in sight. A bird's egg dropped from a nest and smashed into a near-by puddle, making Clara jump. He did not want to leave her alone even to try to get a car or something to take her home, and his perplexity made him restless.

'Will you wait here while I get my car?' he asked running his hand gently through her hair.

'No, don't leave me alone here. There's a path back to the house from here and it's not far. If you help me I can manage to walk back.'

He stood up and looked down at her unable to hide his distress. Clara forced a smile and held out both arms to him. Taking them firmly he helped her to her feet. For a moment she leant against the tree, her mouth firm with determination.

'How do you feel?'

'Not too bad,' she said testing her left ankle by waggling her foot.

'Can you walk?'

'Is my ankle cut badly?'

'Nothing very serious fortunately. Put your arm round my shoulder like this.' He stooped slightly and took her firmly round the waist.

'Now try,' he said.

'I was lucky, I suppose.'

'Yes, you were,' he said concentrating on whether she would walk without restarting the bleeding. She took a step forward using his shoulder and the tree as supports. A stabbing pain in her left hip made her stiffen.

'I hope I haven't broken anything,' she said rubbing her waist just below where Dr Kawa's hand was.

He wished he was big and strong and could have carried her in his arms, but the idea seemed absurd. Presently Clara threw her shoulders back, her head erect, and with his help began the limp home. Though her eyes had the dispossessed look of someone on her way to execution, something in her expression seemed to dwell on the little things with more intense appreciation. The feel of a man's shoulder, the heat rising from the ground and flooding into her; even the wild flowers took on a new significance. But her eyes stared fixedly as if on a distant calamity which she knew she could not avoid.

'What a beautiful day,' she said as if it was the last she would ever see.

'It will be just as nice tomorrow and the following day, and the one after that,' Dr Kawa said.

In the hall Annie changed from tears to surprise when she saw them arrive in a sideways embrace; and followed surprise with terror at the sight of the blood-soaked handkerchiefs round Clara's ankle.

'More Wahalla! – more tragedy!' she gasped rolling her eyes epileptically towards the ceiling and lifting her arms in symbolic surrender.

'Nothing much, Annie. Only a few cuts. Bring some hot water upstairs in a bowl, will you?' Dr Kawa said. Sufficiently reassured about Clara, Annie defiantly barred their progress across the hall.

'It's Master, Doctor,' Annie said.

'Well?'

'He's gone. Gon'way,' she sobbed resting on the lowest rung of the stairs.

'Gone where?'

'Just gone,' she said waving her arms vaguely and shrugging her shoulders. Annie wiped her eyes with her apron and told her tale.

'Ah was . . . Ah was out pickin' peppers in the garden,' she said between sobs. 'When he come out wi'thout his trousers!' Clara gasped. ''Alf naked like de day 'e was bonn. 'E 'as a hat on 'is head and a walking-stick. Ah did not believe Ah was seeing right. As God is me witness you could 'ave knocked me flat wit' a feader! 'E stand dere in de sun for one minute or so. "Annie" 'E says, "It's such a beautiful day and I'm going for a walk." An' off 'e goes. I tried to stop 'im; God knows. But an ole woman like me!' Annie struggled to her feet and sobbed afresh.

Clara buried her face in her hands and limped up the stairs. When they were on the landing the telephone rang and Dr Kawa picked up the receiver.

'He's all right. The police have found him. He's been taken to Kissy,' he told her.

'That's the lunatic asylum, isn't it?'

'It's the Mental Hospital,' he corrected.

'Hospital yes; but they are not treated, are they?'

'That's not quite correct,' he said making an effort to speak calmly. 'He will be under observation for a while, during which time it will be decided whether to start him on some treatment . . . or . . . or . . .'

'Or let him rot,' she concluded. Insanity was cause for bitter shame. Indelible stigma.

Back in bed again Clara relived the episode at the cemetery with heightened consciousness. Visions of the caved-in features of her lover with herself crouched helplessly in his grave made her shudder so that her teeth chattered furiously, as if in an attack of ague.

Clara tossed her head restlessly from side to side as the kaleidoscope of her life unveiled before her. She saw her husband during his illness when she had nursed him back to health with so much tenderness. She saw again his overwhelming goodness and gratitude towards her which she had come to despise and then to hate; a self-destructive goodness. Had she really changed? Had she become so cruel? Why? Was it that she had changed worlds too suddenly, too blindly, too soon? Had she not given herself enough time to inherit the immunities of the new fevers? How could one ask forgiveness for the ruin of other lives? Forgiveness from whom? There was only oneself and one's relationships to others to account for.

Dr Kawa attended to her ankle. Holding her toes in his hand he cleaned off the crusts of blood as gently as he could. He squeezed her foot unconsciously, admiring her ankle and foot. Why did so much beauty go to waste? How was the vast haemorrhage of the goodness in people and life to be stopped? – the constant oozing away of the marrow and the fragrance – how was it to be prevented? He remembered wryly what Mr McGregor had said jokingly at the school; that the strength of a society lay in its womenfolk. Women – his mind echoed, women, pure simple and fresh. Women that were not ashamed to have breasts – women who understood their vital place in life and did not starve themselves because they wanted to look like men. Let the men look after politics and high finance and railway engines – let the men take a peep at the moon.

Clara withdrew her foot quickly as the iodine smarted. Dr Kawa apologized and searched in his mind for the links of his broken chain of thought. Yes, he said to himself, I was thinking about men and women.

'I haven't any dressings in my bag. I must get some and an injection or two. I won't be long. Will you be all right?' he said to Clara. She nodded. He moved closer and took her arm and felt the heat flowing through the smooth brown skin. Behind the mercury of her eyes he observed the fading zeal and the primordial question which glared like a star out of a bleak sky; 'Why'. He turned hurriedly towards the door so that she would not see the emotion which the same question brought to his face, and almost ran out of the room. He was new to this kind of pain. He found it both bitter and warming. In his profession he had found it necessary to employ a synthetic brand of

160

sympathy which he had found adequately comforted his patients and protected his own sensitivity; but with Clara it was different.

While he was away Clara lay quite still in bed. Like a patient under spinal anaesthetic who in a sense feels more intensely the horror of her amputation because although it is done painlessly she is able to watch the dismembering of her body, Clara continued the dissection of her past life without fuss or conscious resentment. She was startled by the very clarity of her thoughts which grew in objectivity because they flourished in a dispassionate and honest atmosphere. *What has gone wrong with my life?* The sharing of one's talents had always seemed to her a necessary aim in life, and that was what she had tried to do with her physical talents. She asked herself the question which she had hedged every day of her life since her first surrender to Freddie – *have I been happy? I have been offered a glittering life; one that was gay and coated with honey and cream. I have merely licked off the coating and thrown the core into the rubbish heap. Too much.*

Takes all one's time to lick at the outer coating without ever getting to the kernel. What's inside? I shall never know. There may be a pearl at the centre; on the other hand there may be maggots. Maggots! In that case it would be better not to get to the centre at all. To accept the risk of losing the pearl.

All the extenuating circumstances of her life, the advent of material abundance were not enough to account for her moral diarrhoea. *It is enough to say that I could not help it. No; I knew what I was doing and had the power to change my life – to reconsider my direction but I chose not to. I enjoyed the loose griping feeling of the diarrhoea. There's no one to blame; no circumstances; no Almighty; just me.*

Dr Kawa returned and gave her the injections.

'I'll be all right now; please leave me alone,' she said

when he finished dressing her wounds. 'You have enough to do without spending all your time here.' Her voice shook with a mild irritation which offended Dr Kawa.

He packed his consulting bag slowly not knowing whether it was the opportune moment to enter into her life fully. His decision wavered between his own longing which was also bound up with a desire to save Clara from destruction of which he felt he alone was capable, and the iron logic of the circumstances. He fumbled and dropped the scissors on the bed in the vain hope that his mind would be able to decide in that extra minute which he spent looking for them among the bedclothes, but it was not enough. There was never enough time to come to terms with oneself. Clara turned her face towards the wall and waited to hear his departing footsteps, but they did not go. The blood rushed to her head, and she tried to swallow the lump which sat in her throat. *Why doesn't he go?* She clutched the bedclothes and pressed her thighs together firmly feeling emotion between them. Clara rolled over on to her back suddenly piercing his ardour with the cautery of her eyes. Her breasts rose and fell above the turmoil of her heart.

'You have been very kind; now please go,' she said. Dr Kawa moved a pace forward, his thighs pressed hard against the bed. The futility of words; the confused adventuring of thought.

Clara's cheeks ached with the spasm of her muscles as she clung to her bed now that her whole life had been battened to the earth. She wanted desperately to weep but could not find the tears; to shout out, but her voice seemed to have withered away. Struggling in the nightmarish impotence of her will, she saw herself in a hay-field with lush grass growing from her head, and her pulse beating in concert with the warm furrowed ground. A vast and kindly sky of perfect blueness opened above her and she longed to embrace it, to wash herself in its transparent pureness, but the rift between them was too great. She belonged to the earth and she must yield herself to it completely. Spreading out her legs under the bed-clothes she writhed, rolled and buried herself in the hay with which she felt an affinity. When she had finished her rape of the field, Dr Kawa was still standing there like a child waiting to be kissed before going to bed.

'Go . . . go now, please,' she said.

He understood her only too well. Like a patient await-ing death, only wanting to be left in peace. In its harsh simplicity it was the final gratitude, well meant, like the cheque left in the will for an illness he had failed to cure. He turned and left the room.

Annie was waiting red-eyed in the hall leaning against the cream panelling, the grizzly stubs on her chin wet with tears. Her dislike of Clara had never taken root and was nothing more than an intense disapproval of her life. This feeling was now softened into concern and pity. She could see the pattern of disintegration of the family turning full circle because she believed that God was not a Borrower but a Lender who always punished the variant life.

'Well, how's Misses?' she asked Dr Kawa who peered at her through the mistiness of his gaze. He walked towards her, staring at her myopically and, taking Annie's chubby arm in his hand he spoke with all his weight behind his voice.

'Stay by her,' he said. 'Don't hate her.'

'Don't hurt yourse'f for nottin',' she told him as he went out through the door. She turned and walked up the stairs which led to Clara's room.

*   *   *   *

163

Flames crackle where the bush is dry. Dr Kawa was not surprised to find his mother waiting for him when he got home. In fact he had been expecting her to raise hell for a long time. His visits to the old house had become noticeably fewer during the strenuous weeks he had been through, and the longer it went on the more difficult it was for him to face her 'serious talk' as she called it. It could not be helped that she had chosen the worst possible moment.

Mrs Kawa was sitting in an arm-chair as he went in through the door. He kissed her on the forehead and sprawled on the settee with every mark of physical and mental exhaustion. She noticed the new lines on his face which reflected the strain of his life, and although this worried her, she managed to crease her cheeks in a compassionate smile. She had not seen him for three days but had shared all his agonies and had done what she believed was her proper duty as a mother to smooth the path of his life. When Mrs Kawa had first noticed Clara's influence she had consulted 'Daddy Alpha'.

Daily, before the Rhode Island cock crew or the morning mist had lifted, Mrs Kawa had nimbled her way to the ramshackle house at the bottom of the street, near the three-pronged avenue of orange trees which sheltered Government House, and the ancient Cotton Tree. There, on the steps, she had left a bowl of rice, eggs and cola nuts, the latter kept fresh in banana-leaf wrappings; and backed away through the twanging of the metal gate even before the mangy dog had pricked its ears and decided that there was no cause for alarm. She hurried home keeping close to the fences in case anyone should see her, and on reaching home fell on her knees and prayed for her son's deliverance from the snare of the devil Clara. Daddy Alpha, who was expected to wind protective spells round Dr Kawa, lived well off her generosity and got himself up handsomely in a Khaftan of white muslin which Mrs Kawa had produced to urge the spell – she had even slaughtered a sheep and distributed the mutton to all and sundry. Yet the more expensively she tried to protect her son, the deeper he appeared to become embroiled. In the end the old man had confessed that her son was no ordinary person, and that he had a strong head which all the powers of the old man's art could not influence. He had therefore advised Mrs Kawa to have a talk with her son. He had done all he could by way of preparing the ground – it was now left to her to employ a mother's persuasiveness.

This had prompted her to call on her son, and considering him with sidelong glances Mrs Kawa braced herself for the attack.

'You don't look at all well, boy,' she began.

'I am a bit run down, I suppose.'

'You have not been sleeping.' The question and statement in her voice only produced the shadow of a smile on his face but he said nothing.

'How is Grannie May?' she asked, giving him time to erase the lines of irritation gathering at the corners of his eyes.

'She'll be away for a while, I'm afraid. That chest of hers isn't the latest model,' he replied introducing a lighter note into the conversation.

'Is the houseboy managing all right?'

'He's very good – one hardly notices Grannie May's absence. In fact I am wondering if she ought to bother to come back.'

'You must have a woman in the house.'

Dr Kawa moved uneasily on the settee. For the second time within an hour he was faced with making a decision and felt he lacked the strength to do so; he took the easy way out and procrastinated.

'I saw Mrs Coker last week,' his mother said casually.

'Who is she?' he asked absentmindedly.

'You know! Mrs Coker who came here some time ago with some other women.'

'Oh yes! I remember. It was quite amusing.'

'Amusing? How amusing?'

'She was the one who was so keen to get me married wasn't she?'

'I don't see anything amusing about that,' said Mrs Kawa, cancelling the humorous note in her son's voice with a stern and almost querulous one in hers. She made herself comfortable in her chair.

'In fact there's no mother worth her salt who does not wish to see her son married. I don't say to the first girl who comes along showing her breasts like words of wisdom, but you can't live like this all your life. It won't lead to any good.' He spied at her through the corners of his eyes and cleared his throat nervously. The collision seemed imminent but he tried a last and desperate manœuvre to avert it.

'I'm tired, Ma,' he said half appealingly. 'Besides I'm old enough—'

'Men are never old enough,' she shouted before he could finish his sentence, and struck the arm of her chair. There was a brief silence. Composed again, she leaned towards him and spoke in a pleading tone, hoping to appeal to his reason as well as his conscience.

'Look here boy. I am your mother. You are all I have left in the world. I don't want to fight with you; but who will tell you the truth if I don't? Don't think that I don't know about this woman.' She pointed carelessly over her shoulder at the house next door and a disparaging scowl crept into her eyes.

'She is beautiful but she is nothing but Wahalla and ruin. You have seen what she has done to her husband. Such a good man. We won't have her in our family,' she concluded. Her eyes flashed with a fury not directed against her son but at the debris of her crumbling ambition for him.

'I love her,' he said, almost meekly.

'I can't help that, but that's as far as it will go.'

'I love her,' he repeated passionately as he sat up and squeezed all his reserves of energy into the words. 'I can see the whole destructive genius of her life, yet I love her.'

'You can love her without selling yourself to her.'

'I love her and she needs help. I must stay by her; help her.'

Mrs Kawa hissed a slow sizzling hiss which she reserved for those moments of crisis when she felt the ground moving under her feet. She saw that his love was adulterated with pity, and this consoled her a little. So impure a passion added to his natural reflectiveness would allow her time to get to work again on breaking the alliance; but unwilling to expose her new source of strength, she pretended desperation and got off her chair brusquely.

'You will never have her. You will not profit by raising a mother's wrath against you,' she said shaking a vehement finger at him. He approached her. An argument with his mother was the most hateful thing to him and now it had happened, he felt limp with remorse.

'Let me drive you home, Ma. I've got to go to Kissy,' he said. His mother took him by both arms and shook him firmly.

'Don't let this whole house fall on your head boy.

167

Promise me. Swear to me,' she pleaded with tears in her eyes.

'She's no ordinary woman. Why should she go to waste?' he asked.

'My son is no ordinary boy either. She made her bed and now she must lie down in it; and you are not going to interfere with God's punishment. Promise me boy! Promise me.'

He was torn between rebellion and submission but his doughty emotions prevailed. He remembered that a man's strength lay in avoiding open battle with a woman on her own domain, and a broken smile crossed his face.

'Anything you say, Ma,' he said, leading her out to the car. A sudden freshness came into Mrs Kawa's eyes as if she had shed a heavy burden.

'We aren't licked yet; my boy and I,' she thought as they drove into town.

It was the whining of the engine and the automatic change into low gear which made Dr Kawa realize that he was already climbing the secluded hill of Kissy. Forming a sort of parapet at the top, the sinister red brick walls of the Asylum loomed high against the sky as if hanging from it. Dr Kawa's spirits always sank when he saw the jagged line of glass spikes along the top of the surrounding walls, and he had conveniently conditioned himself never to think about the place and its inmates until he arrived there.

He looked at the green iron gate, towering above him which two strong sinewy porters were beginning to swing open when they recognized his car, and his throat went dry. Sighing with despair, he did not even acknowledge their salutes as he let off the hand-brake and crawled through the gates into the desolate world of the insane.

He parked his car at the opposite end of the quadrangle and for a moment lacked the courage to leave it. The Lay Superintendent in a khaki uniform came bounding down the steps towards him, his corpulent belly swinging jauntily in front of him.

'Hello, Doc,' the superintendent said labouring the 'Doc' with undisguised sarcasm. He knew well enough that none of the doctors who looked after the patients at the Asylum had any special training or qualifications for the job, and that they felt as though they were walking on slime when they were within the walls of his castle. Thus he delighted to add to their uneasiness. He had a way of jerking his mole's head, a caricature on his massively built body, which irritated Dr Kawa. The superintendent had once told Dr Kawa point-blank that insanity was the punishment inflicted on hen-pecked husbands and wives in trousers and as such his 'college students' as he referred to the inmates with inverted humour, deserved little care and less of doctors.

'I would like to see . . .' Dr Kawa began trying to establish a professional relationship with the superintendent but was not allowed to finish.

'Marshall?' shouted the burly man with the tiny head. 'I've been expecting this for a long time. Frankly I thought that bitch of his would get here first,' he continued.

Dr Kawa froze in his steps and his fingers curled involuntarily into a fist, but he realized nothing would be gained by goading the hulk of the other for a tender spot.

'Will you show me to the patient?' he said calmly and stiffly.

'Yes, I'll take you to Marshall myself. Number four cell.'

Dr Kawa squirmed at the thought which the superintendent's reference prompted. *How quickly a man loses identity here. Take this asylum with all its wretchedness under an inane monster of a superintendent and multiply it several million times and the product is the world we live in. What is it about this place? It is the pig-swill odours and the faecal marks on the walls, the neglected men and women under a rule of terror which sickens me?*

They were half-way up the steps to the main body of the building. An old woman sat with a blank expression on the edge of a step, her grey tresses floating on her shoulders. She was unconcernedly mixing a brown paste in her left palm with her right index finger and putting her finger to her lips. Then she smeared the paste over her cheeks, lips and brow. Without looking at Dr Kawa she raised the smeared finger towards him on the skinny prop of her arm as they went past.

'Share with me the body and blood of Satan,' she said. The wounding smell of faeces reached him from the finger and appeasing his stomach with gulped mouthfuls of air, he hurried up the short flight of steps and disappeared into the closed corridor.

On the steps the superintendent considered the old woman fiercely while she continued to hold out her arm which was beginning to tremble with fatigue as she stared into space. Angered because the old woman did not appear to be aware of his towering presence much less of the dictates of his expression, he struck her on the side of the face with the back of his hand. The old woman rolled off the steps and lay motionless in the sand. A wiry man nearing seventy who had been officiating at an imaginary baptism at one end of the quadrangle ran to her aid. On reaching her however, he had forgotten the feelings of anxiety which had prompted his action, and overjoyed at finding a real candidate, recommenced the Order of Service, shedding tears for her salvation.

Meanwhile the superintendent strode after Dr Kawa who had walked down the aisle between the caged screamers. He nodded to the warder pacing up and down with a menacing clatter of hob-nailed boots who pointed out number four cell with his truncheon.

Mr Marshall sat close against the wall on his straw mattress seemingly content with his coarse pair of institution pyjamas. An enamel wash-basin, empty except for the ring of dirt which the previous occupant had left, decked a small table opposite. The familiar smell of straw and bedbugs thickened the air and made it difficult for Dr Kawa to breathe.

Looking round at the inmates behind iron bars, Dr Kawa felt smitten by guilt. One woman sat throttling herself and would continue to press her fingers round her throat until she dropped unconscious; would recover, and start all over again.

God knows it isn't criminal negligence on my part; just the sheer frustration of ignorance.

The superintendent threw severe glances at the warders who slammed to attention as he careered by with the crowing confidence of a man who has done his good turn for the day, and even suspects it will last out a week.

'Well Doc!' the superintendent boomed jovially on arrival in his castrato voice for which Dr Kawa was secretly grateful. He tried to imagine what the superintendent would be like with a voice proportionate to his size, and shuddered at the thought.

The twice wound lock clicked and the hinges squeaked. A ray of recognition spurted from Mr Marshall's eyes but soon disappeared, as the clouds shut out the sun in

October. Yet he seemed to understand the superintendent's dumb speech and stood up meekly like a frightened schoolboy.

Dr Kawa walked up to him and resting a hand on his shoulder, forced him to sit down.

'Leave us alone,' he said to the superintendent without looking at him. The superintendent braced his shoulder, drew in a deep breath and walked out of the cell but stood outside the door.

'Will you go away?' Dr Kawa said raising his voice. The superintendent looked round quickly to see if any of the warders had witnessed the insult before he stamped away in a rage, ordering a warder to keep an eye on number four.

Alone with Mr Marshall at last, Dr Kawa sat tongue-tied for what seemed a circle of moments. His heart was full of a mixture of feelings which he could not crystallize into words. Mr Marshall on the other hand seemed either unaware of or indifferent to the other's presence. Sitting with his hands between his thighs knocking his knees together he was completely engrossed in a whole new world of his own. But instead of concentrating on what he was trying to formulate in his mind, Dr Kawa found that he could not rid it of a few lines of poetry which irritated him because of their irrelevance to the situation in hand; and also because he could not remember where they came from or who had written them.

> *Let the fishes eat their straw*
> *And the cows gorge their udders*
> *With sea-weed and salt spray . . .*

Worst of all, now that he was concentrating on the poem he could not remember any more of it – perhaps it wasn't a poem at all! What was poetry? Rhyme? Truth glossed over in words? Escape? Unreality? Insanity?

'Jackie!' he said. 'You won't be here long.' The idea made him feel better and his breathing became easier. Yes, he would get Jackie home, even past that rock of a superintendent and he and Clara would look after him together. The forlorn hope gleamed that perhaps Clara in the rebirth of her tragedy would dedicate to her husband the final instalment of her love. Love, life, what did it matter? They were one and the same thing. He would go straight to the superintendent and declare Mr Marshall discharged. No, wait a minute – was he perhaps too involved personally in a professional matter? Yes; it would be wiser to go through the rigmarole of a second opinion. Yes, that would be the thing to do. Meanwhile he would get Jackie transferred upstairs to the doctor's room which was never used. He got up to leave.

'You've brought Sonia!' Mr Marshall said with a mixture of gratitude and endearment, his eyebrows raised as he seemed to be looking through Dr Kawa into the more acute world of his imagination. Dr Kawa shook his head.

'But it won't be long before you see her again,' he said.

'You have her round the corner there,' Mr Marshall insisted, stooping to peer between Dr Kawa's legs.

'Put that knife down, Sonia,' he said, pointing his • finger warningly. Suddenly he screamed and threw himself back on his bed with his hands shielding his face from some horrifying spectacle. So genuine was the contortion and terror in his face that Dr Kawa involuntarily swung round although he knew that there was no one else there except the warder down the corridor.

He opened his bag, fetched out and filled a syringe and injected the fluid into the bulge of Mr Marshall's shoulder.

He helped him into bed and waited to see him fall asleep before he left.

The warder sprang forward to lock the door.

'There's no need for that; he's not dangerous. I've given him an injection which will make him sleep for several hours,' Dr Kawa said.

'My orders to lock up all prisoners, sir,' the warder replied bracing his shoulders with military discipline. With surreptitious glances towards the superintendent's office he indicated that he could not take so grave a responsibility on his own shoulders.

'Blast your orders,' Dr Kawa shouted losing his patience. But it had the desired effect. A genial smile fractured the stern veneer of the warder's face and Mr Marshall's cell was left unlocked.

When Dr Kawa reached the superintendent's office the huge body leaned forward over the table so that the head seemed as though it would roll off on to the papers on the table. The superintendent had purported to rise from his chair. Within these mouldy walls he was supreme and the doctors were not to be encouraged to forget the fact.

'I've given him an injection. These tablets are to be given three times a day,' Dr Kawa said leaving a bottle of sedatives on the table.

'Dr Freeman will be coming to see him – meanwhile you can let him wander about.'

'Never! Never!' the superintendent cackled with flapping lips, his eyes half-way down his cheeks with indignation. 'Never have they been h'allowed outside their cell for seven days. Not until the case is decided – orders, Doctor,' said he searching for his book of rules. The irony of the physical giant with the bird's voice who lived under orders and for orders cut a pathetic picture.

'I prefer to give the orders about my patients,' he said simply.

The underdeveloped lower jaw dropped on to the superintendent's chest. His eyes flashed from Dr Kawa to his own fingers which were being flexed and extended in turn nervously on the table. He was not accustomed to such acts of self-control, and the sweat poured down his face as he slumped back in his chair like a sack of flour.

'Another thing,' said Dr Kawa, 'I want him transferred to the Doctors' room upstairs – my responsibility,' and walked out.

The old woman still sat on the spot where she had fallen and with bowed head received the repeated blessings of the old man.

Someone was shouting out his name at the main gate. Over the top of his car he saw a woman gesticulating frantically from the other side of the gate. He recognized her as Mr Marshall's sister and waved back. He got into his car and drove towards the gate. While two porters swung the gate open a third walked up to the car and shouted through the window.

'She says she is the sister of number four. She been givin' us hell. Muss be in fambly,' he said screwing his index finger into his temple.

'I've only just heard,' she said stepping into the car beside Dr Kawa.

'Rather devastating,' he replied.

'How is he?'

'Asleep at the moment.'

'Is . . . is . . . he wild?'

'Not a bit. On the contrary. He's withdrawn.'

'Such disgrace.'

'There's nothing disgraceful about illness,' he said.

'But you know what people are like. The stigma will stick to the family for ever. Sonia will not marry because her father has . . . well you know,' 'Sister' said.

'Shall I drive you home? There's no point in your going to see him now.' The car slid down the hill.

'I knew it would end like this! Shame and disgrace. What will happen now?' Dr Kawa understood that she was hinting at the rumours concerning himself and Clara as well as inquiring after her brother.

'Well, I shall try to get him home where he can be properly looked after,' he replied.

'The evil power of women,' she sighed.

'It's not only women – women don't have a monopoly of evil in the world you know. Some people crack up because of an idea.'

'An idea? What ideas did Jackie have except to make her happy? Jackie is a simple man, Dr Kawa. He and I grew up together and I have tried to understand his point of view all along. He's not one for ideas – that I know.'

'It hasn't been easy for you, either,' he said sympathetically.

'Easy? With four children to bring up; easy? Believe me, I have had to change myself into a completely new person. I have thought and done things which would have never occurred to me when my husband was alive. But Jackie would not budge. He thought his love was like the hills or the stars . . . could survive everything. He never understood how to make a compromise. Look at him now.'

'That was his great idea for which you and I can perhaps feel proud. He believed in his love. He believed it was all powerful – stronger than any human knowledge or experience. He believed it was stronger than self-destruction, but he did not understand the mechanics of it, nor was he strong enough for the experiment he set himself. In a sense he was a pioneer – a stray seed which will find root in some dark craggy hillside one day. But I am sorry to sound so much like a philosopher.'

'You talk as if he were dead,' she challenged.

'The Jackie we used to know is dead,' he said.

It was already evening when Dr Kawa turned his car off the side road into the main Port Loko road. A mixture of the smells of cooking and flowers was wafted to his nostrils and made him a little cheerful. Spindles of red light strained in the sky as if suspending the red ball which was rolling over the hills to the westward. Hope fired up in Dr Kawa as he watched a chain of clouds amble east. The evening train hooted and smoked its way into Freetown, its carriages bulging with vegetables.

Dr Kawa was very tired. His eyes smarted with fatigue while the muscles of his arms contracted under his shirt. He drove slowly along the empty road past the stone quarries on the left and the bakery with its heart-warming smell of hot bread. 'Sister' sat quietly beside him taking in the pleasant air and not thinking about anything in particular.

'Shall I drive you home? I'm calling to see Sonia at the Convent. I said I would,' Dr Kawa said.

'You've done very well for the child. It's a good thing the other one went to Fernando Po. I would like to come with you.'

In the hall at the Convent, Sister Georgette was pacing up and down to the telling of her rosary. At the sound of approaching footsteps she ran to the door to see if Dr Kawa had arrived, and had been mistaken so often that when he did walk through the door she did not immediately recognize him.

'Doctor! Doctor!' she whispered bravely when she recognized him and approached him with her habit modestly raised. He quickened his pace to take her hand.

'Sonia? Lord have mercy!' 'Sister' exclaimed drawing her own conclusion from the look on Sister Georgette's face. Sister Georgette was one of those living martyrs who lose sight of their former objectives in life. Selfless to a fault in her everyday dealings, she compensated for the exacting demands on her life by a solemn expression which reflected a considerable degree of suffering. Almost imperceptible lines brush-stroked her face and told of the channels along which she smiled in her youth.

'Nothing's happened yet,' she said reassuringly to Dr Kawa.

'Is she unwell? Is she not behaving herself?' he asked.

'I sincerely hope my fears are unjustified, but Doctor I've never been so frightened about a child before. She's odd. Well you know what she's been like and what she's been through, poor child! For two days she has refused to eat anything, and last night I had to go to her bed three times because she was screaming in her sleep. Each time she was drenched in sweat, her hands clenched, and she was shaking like a leaf.'

Dr Kawa listened calmly but 'Sister' grimaced in the background as if she knew everything before it was told.

'A few hours ago she became so tearful – you never saw anything like it. Whatever is the matter with her? She's not happy here, Doctor.' Concluding thus, Sister Georgette allowed her impassive features to explain that she was at her wits' end, and that she entertained dreadful forebodings about the child.

'Come and see her,' she said at length.

They were led into a small but cosy sitting-room on the ground floor.

Sonia was sitting in an arm-chair like an old woman, holding up her head with both hands, her legs stretched out in front of her. She did not move when they entered the room. Her eyes were unflinching and still wet with tears. Sister Georgette raised her eyebrows and a gentle question invaded her eyes; but Sonia remained seated, and although she was staring straight at them, did not show any signs of recognition.

Her aunt rushed up to her, taking the child's face in her hands. Stooping slightly, she brought her face level with Sonia's so that they looked into each other's eyes. Sonia's lips pouted between the vice of her aunt's grip, but still she did not move.

'Poor child! Do you want to come home with me?'

Sister Georgette glanced at Dr Kawa forbidding the aunt's suggestion.

'I want to go home,' Sonia said with a firmness too mature for her age.

'Sister' withdrew shrugging her shoulders and Dr Kawa moved forward and crouched in front of the child taking her hand in his. He decided to speak plainly to her as he would to an adult.

'Sonia dear, your papa has gone away for a few days and your mama isn't well. There's only Annie to look after you at home. Would you like to come and stay with me for a few days?' Scarcely had he made the offer than he regretted doing so. *I'm in no better position to look after her myself.* Sonia stared at him as though she could read his thoughts.

'I want to go home,' she insisted.

'Aren't you happy here?' he asked caressing her hand gently.

'I want to go home.'

'Home it is then,' he said rising.

Sonia grabbed her raffia bag while Dr Kawa took her case.

Back in the hall a little girl younger than Sonia ran up breathless and tongue-tied.

'What is it child?' Sister Georgette asked.

'Th . . . Th . . . Sister Ber . . . Ber . . . Bernard said – her . . . her said to tell you . . . th . . th . . not knife found,' she blurted.

'Sister Bernard wants me to know that the knife has not been found.' The little girl nodded extravagantly and ran off.

'They've lost a knife in the kitchen. They're always doing that,' Sister Georgette explained.

'God Bless,' she said as they went through the door.

Soon after they heard her lock it hastily as if Satan himself was forcing an entry.

'Perhaps I'd better come with you – for the child's sake,' 'Sister' volunteered as they drove away.

When they got home Annie was there to smother Sonia with affection and to commiserate with 'Sister'. Dr Kawa was anxious to know how Clara was, and gave Annie news of Mr Marshall in exchange. While they were thus engaged Sonia ran up the stairs and halted in front of Clara's bedroom. Her young face contracted in pain as she held her raffia bag to her chest. She entered the room silently.

Clara lay on her back with her face turned to the wall, asleep. Tears rolled down Sonia's face. She clutched her handbag with both hands and rushed towards the bed. She leaned with all her strength on her mother. Clara swung her head round and her body shook as she pulled her knees up automatically. She pressed the convulsed body of her child more closely and firmly to her own. Her fingers clutched and released Sonia's coat in turns and her eyes faded in a paroxysm of pain.

Dr Kawa and 'Sister' entered the room. He ran to the bedside at seeing the anguish on Clara's face.

'Don't lean on Mummy; Mummy's not well,' he said trying to pull Sonia away, but Clara clung to her child desperately. He seized Sonia in a fit of panic and wrenched her away. The little raffia handbag was stained with blood. Uncomprehending he tried to lift the bag but it was anchored firmly, and inside it he felt the handle of a knife.

Chapter Eleven

Today's green grass is tomorrow's hay; Sunday was bright and happy with bells as the immature tones from the village churches vied with the self-conscious chimes from the Cathedral; and as their question and answer grew into an agitated rumble, the air became dizzy under the clear sky.

The birds too were like choristers engrossed in the magic of a new piece of music even before they were familiar with it. Swaying smoothly on feeble branches, they pecked at and preened their feathers excitedly as they prepared to lift themselves on the crests of their high spirits into the luminous softness of a beautiful day.

Down among the roots of the hedge-plants snails slimed their bodies and crawled about with characteristic aimlessness.

The geranium and hibiscus poked their heads from under the leaves of shadowless green as children do through doors when there are guests in the house.

Everything was gay and brilliant with the fascination of life and the outpouring of goodness. Leaping frollicking, rolling, cajoling nature shook the air with warmth and affection and spurned the gloomy and taciturn days under Libra so that everything was injected with an ebullience in reaction to the repression of recent days.

Even the mangy dog down the road seemed to have come to an agreement with the flies, and stretched himself out indifferently under the citrous shades where he was sprinkled with feathery lights, and cast langorous eyes at the darting shadows of the leaves which played mischievously on the white-washed tree trunk in front of him.

This was the day following Clara's death, which like an avalanche growing at the expense of the path it chooses had involved a number of lives in the confusion of its wilfulness. On such a day the industry of nature might have declared its bankruptcy and the world come to an end as prophesied by the latest seer Ada Jobi. But the world did not end, and indeed had no intention of doing so. The people of Freetown shed crocodile tears for Clara and forgot her.

'That's one disease cured,' they thought.

But the evil of an infectious disease is not judged by the absolute fatalities but by the potential fatalities; suffering and bitterness are not significant because of their numerical incidence but because they contaminate the pure cultures of a society at peace with itself. The people of Freetown did not reflect that a society at peace with itself, like its individual members, or the organs within the individual or more minutely still, the cells of which such organs are composed, can only function with brilliance and health because their inner harmony is ensured. If one needs air in order to be oneself, the Self is equally determined by the composition of the air it breathes. The waste bag of experience continues to bulge inconsequentially.

On that morning when the air glowed with so much pride and a sense of the continuance of things, Freetown society limped along like a dog with a thorn in its paw, snarling from political motives and determinedly abandoning itself to pleasure.

Dr Kawa lay in bed with his head supported in his hands, staring in the intensely reflective mood in which he had gone to bed the previous night. He had not slept, but when the smoky beam peered through the curtains he knew it was morning.

He heard the low drawling of the 'wakers' from next door. They had sung all night round Clara so as to soften the journey of the spirit of the dead to its new life beyond. Because of the absence of male voices he supposed that the numbers had dwindled and he visualized the wakers with their cups of black coffee in one hand and brandy glasses in the other, their aged heads dropping on their shoulders with the weight of sleep, but all the time chanting the traditional hymns and songs with dispossessed voices. Occasionally as if wakened from a frightening dream, a shrill voice would wail evocatively, and the stalling engine of the chorus would jerk forwards to another standstill.

The thought of the mourners drinking coffee and brandy to keep them 'fired' and awake pleased him, because he had provided the brandy so that Clara would at least be laid out with people around her.

He saw Clara in his mind's eye lying motionless in her white dress, a flower garlanded with roses. He saw the heavy eyebrows like rain-clouds which had filled him with such longing, and the steady brown of her skin. He remembered the whimsical smile tinged with a vain pleading which had driven away the agony of dying. He threw his mind back deeper into an earlier succession of time to the Clara he never knew but whose image he now conceded was the object of his love. He no longer fought against or rejected the thought.

Clara as she appeared to him was sitting on the ground by a well in her own village with her legs crossed under her. She was looking out towards the gardens, a sparkle of green, yellow and red, where the women with their infants strapped to their backs tended the vegetables. She looked as native as the soil, warmly spirited with the sophistication of innocence. She faced the rising sun. Dr Kawa sat up suddenly in bed as he imagined he saw a snake creeping up behind Clara. He tried desperately to warn her and to slay the serpent simultaneously, but Clara, the snake and the sun-washed vegetable furrows were all part of the same thought picture, and he only succeeded of disposing of one element at the expense of all the rest. He flung himself back on his bed and while he was still wondering about time, he was already asleep.

It was late when he got out of bed feeling even more tired for having slept. His neck muscles ached and he winced when he pulled the curtains back and faced the strong light. Then he staggered back into the sitting-room and walked around the settee aimlessly. Back in the bedroom he put on some clothes and recrossing the sitting-room he opened the front door and stared at a rose bush humming with bees.

He turned sharply as a large shadow which he felt rather than saw came leaping towards him. A large man had left his stony seat in the shade cast by the house and was holding something out to him; was offering him something. Dr Kawa was more dazed and surprised than frightened, and without looking at what the man was offering he studied the face keenly. It was a familiar face and Dr Kawa was conscious of a whole bundle of associations which made the face known to him, but for a long time he could not remember.

The man had on a pair of blue cotton 'Krootos' which hung loose between his legs, and made the enormous bellows-like embellishment fluctuate between his legs as he walked. He half crouched before Dr Kawa as a sign of deference, and with bowed head, his hand on his chest said:

'Turtle made nice for you.'

'Of course. How ridiculous not to have recognized you, Sori. Thank you very much,' he said accepting the present. He held the large charger of the turtle's breast-plate in both hands overcome with gratitude. The workmanship was exquisite. The rim was sheathed neatly in red Moroccan leather, and around the silver turtle with which the centre was embossed the rest of the base was inlaid with threads of leather woven into symbolic images.

Dr Kawa raised it high in the open doorway as a priest would the offertory, and happy tears welled into his eyes. Such an act of dedication was just what he needed at that moment to revive him from the pain and confusion of Clara's death.

'But this is very expensive; how much?'

Sori gesticulated with hurt feelings. 'Is f'you,' he said emphatically as if he was talking to a deaf person.

'Yes, but I must pay for it. You have spent a lot of money on it.'

'Money no matter,' Sori said waving his large hand with finality. Dr Kawa rotated the shield so that he could see the four inlaid figures at each corner in turn, and he nodded and shook his head with sheer amazement.

'What do these figures mean? What do they represent?' he asked Sori as he saw the eager excitement in the other's eyes. Sori took a hurried step towards him and looked at the design over Dr Kawa's shoulder. His large teeth thrust his lips apart and an open smile swept his face as he pointed to the images in turn.

'Dis; woman insaid hegg.' *Woman inside egg.*

'Hegg is wold.' *The egg is the world.*

'Why is it blue?' Dr Kawa asked. To this Sori shrugged his shoulders and pointed to the sky.

'Dis man wit spear.' *Man with a spear.*

'Why red?'

'Cause man is sun,' Sori said expanding his broad shoulders.

'Dis; is corn 'cause good cams from groun.' *Green corn sheaves; goodness comes from the soil.*

Dr Kawa raised his head and weighed the sense and depth of the words.

'And this child reaching for the fruit is love,' Dr Kawa suggested, feeling pleased with his interpretation. But an inquiring perplexity, as a child's, came into Sori's expression.

'Loff? What is?' Sori asked, a little ashamed of his ignorance. But he added;

'Child is friendship – all people friends.'

'And the yellow fruit which the child cannot reach?' asked Dr Kawa.

Sori snapped his fingers and bit them. He rolled his head round and round looking from tree to tree with the agonies of a suffocating man. He was trying to recover a word which he hoped to find in the breath of the leaves or the very colour of the tree trunks.

'Allah!' he shouted with frustration, slapping his thigh.

'A golden fruit. What can it mean? A golden fruit and a child reaching for it. Knowledge? Need?' Dr Kawa racked his brain in vain.

'Pass . . . Passiens,' Sori fumbled.

'Patience,' Dr Kawa exploded with delight. The two

men laughed heartily at having seized the word. Sori took the turtle-shell tray from Dr Kawa and leaving his slippers outside tiptoed to the table and left the tray on it. He rejoined Dr Kawa and holding his battered helmet under his arm with bowed head said;

'I solly velly bad.'

But before Dr Kawa could overcome the surge of friendliness towards Sori which choked his throat, Sori was down the drive and out of sight.

Back in his bedroom he threw the window open and watched the acolyte crows in the orange orchard on the other side of the sloping hedge. They lifted their beaks like little candles while the cawing jackdaws spread their wings as they hopped on the branches just over the heads of some mourners who had gone out into the bright fresh morning to shake off the moisture of sleep.

Dr Kawa watched with bleary eyes. He felt an overwhelming desire to sleep; but he did not want to give in to the desire. Throwing an old gaberdine round his shoulders he crossed the sitting-room straightening the edge of the carpet with his foot on the way and spent a moment admiring Sori's present before he went out into the crisp morning.

He skirted the house and quickened his pace towards the narrow path which strayed from between the pepper shrubs at the bottom of his garden, and, confident that no one next door had seen him, settled into a slow meditative walk until he came out to some fields. The land rolled gently towards a railway bridge in the distance. Dr Kawa made for a little brook which had been swollen by the rains so that the powdered rocks which looked like loaves of bread in their hard bed in the dry season, now shone with a polished glaze under the foaming water. Since the moment when he had witnessed Sonia's

matricide and had felt the cold clamp of Clara's hand, Dr
Kawa had searched for an explanation.

When he had felt the handle of the knife hilt-deep in
Clara's body he had withdrawn it with a swift defiance.
Unthinking he had stood watching the blood drip from
the tip for a moment. Then he had pushed the
knife through a hole in the panelling of the room, and
had heard it grate its way down between the concrete
wall and the wood. He had rushed Sonia and her aunt out
of the room and taken upon his shoulders the responsi-
bility of giving it out that Clara had taken her own life.
He could not say why he had done this; he had acted
intuitively. The primary falsehood had inevitably started
off a whole train of other falsehoods. As he walked by the
stream and the first significance of his actions was
exposed to him, actions of less than twenty-four hours
ago now seemed horrific in their error and deceit. He
realized that he had committed a crime. He threw himself
on a mound of green turf and lay there a long time.

Until that moment his concern for events had been so
fixed on the articulate, the tangible, the factual and their
relationship to the emotional and philosophical com-
plexes, that although he had become embroiled in their
shuntings, his own action had been relegated to the other
dimension of passive behaviour. But these actions of his
had suddenly returned like the first wife of a bigamous
marriage, to claim their heritage, and the impact was
similar to the delayed shock which strikes those who have
performed superhuman acts of bravery, only to be struck
down at a moment unrelated in time to their heroism, by
the physical fear to which all men are subject.

He washed his face in the cool water and continued his
walk along the stream. At the bridge he climbed up on to
the main road.

He was now in an abstracted state of mind, not even conscious of the traffic or the canaries twittering from their cages in open windows. From time to time he was not even aware of himself or his movements. Past the hump in the road he came face to face with a noisy celebrating crowd. A few paces plunged him into the merry-making and he pressed through the swaying bodies in an effort to escape from reality, from people, but most of all from the haunting memories of Clara. He groped his way through the sweating bodies, the blackened lips emphasizing the whiteness of the teeth and the succulent rhythm of their skins matching the love-play of their walking dance; arms loosely yet delicately swaying, movements clumsy at their inception but smoothly flowing into each other towards a rounded whole. Heads waving with the restrained frenzy of a flower caught in a breeze; and somewhere in the midst of it all the power which controlled all their suppleness – the soft, cool, untiring breath of the xylophone. The whole excited splendour heightened by the smell of fruit and the heavy breathing of the dancers, the curious broadening of the music of the xylophone augmented by the shouts, the laughter, the occasional stamping, and even the blasts from cars which crawled through the dance, into an intoxicating orchestration, mesmerized him.

Dr Kawa staggered out of it all and found himself standing by the railings on King Tom's bridge overlooking yet another rushing stream a hundred yards below.

He had not been there long when he felt a hand on his shoulder. Startled, he turned round and stared into the beaming face of Mr Hamilton. The pleasure of seeing an old friend had its effect, and he smiled slowly, relieved, vacantly. Mr Hamilton's smile broadened. Dr Kawa shook his hand.

'Shall we walk? I'm going to the school to straighten out one or two things,' Mr Hamilton suggested. 'Lucky I met you,' he prompted.

'How's that?' Dr Kawa replied.

'Well, I was hoping I'd find time to call on you one of these days.'

'I hope not professionally,' Dr Kawa said absent-mindedly.

'No. No . . . Mr Hamilton murmured. 'I thought we would see much more of each other, that's all.'

'One thing and another,' Dr Kawa said.

'I've always felt like a father to you, and I would appreciate it if you could think of me as such. I know that as one gets older one's isolation increases. One no longer feels able to avail oneself of the advice one sometimes needs,' Mr Hamilton said. 'I did want to come and see you as I said; but somehow I could never manage to take that short cut across the fields to your place, and as you know I don't run a car!' he went on.

'I might have come to see you a long time ago, but my problems have been decided, sorted out for me. That seems to be my greatest talent. If I wait long enough everything evens itself out,' Dr Kawa said.

'But not always in the way you'd wish, I dare say.'

'Perhaps not; but one can't bear the suspense of irre-solution too long. Things must go either one way or the other. Compromise is a lie. When it comes to essentials, compromise is deceit and cowardice.'

A new Humber approached at top speed and swerved towards them, mounting the pavement before the driver swung back on to the road, and squealed round the corner and on towards the bridge. The two men had flattened themselves against the tin fence and watched the driver wave at them after giving them such a fright.

'What a curious greeting,' Mr Hamilton said, recovering. 'That boy left school only last year, and they say he's made a lot of illicit money. I suppose he wanted to show off his car. You and I might have served to satisfy his self-esteem,' he said with a macabre chuckle.

Dr Kawa stood suddenly rigid and still, his face lacerated, his eyes like pools of blood.

'What's the matter? Are you all right, boy?' Mr Hamilton shouted as he swung round and faced Dr Kawa. But just as suddenly Dr Kawa's face relaxed and he stepped aside and walked on while Mr Hamilton still peered after him over the top of his crescent spectacles.

'Yes, I'm all right,' Dr Kawa said.

At that very moment Clara was being buried.

'I know you've had a strenuous time, but you shouldn't let things get on top of you. Why don't you take a holiday? Go away for a while,' Mr Hamilton said, lengthening his stride to keep up with Dr Kawa.

'That's exactly what I am going to do. I think I shall go to Bo.'

'That's an idea. Right away. Go to Bo for a month, even two weeks, and you'll be yourself again.'

'I'm asking for a transfer to Bo. A month won't be enough to wash off this stain.'

'Oh! Transfer! I . . . I hadn't contemplated anything quite so drastic.'

'One has to be drastic to survive. Just as kindness never won anything except a smile, so one's sensibilities repay only anguish. I need to get away like a turtle when she has laid her eggs. Perhaps one of the troubles with human beings is that they don't migrate enough these days. They hold on to a little piece of earth, an idea, an emotion, and are ready to see the rest of the world go up in smoke to keep it.'

'But Bo is a long way. Away from your own people.'

'My own people are just any who accept me.'

'You realize Bo is not like Freetown. Not developed.'

'That's what I need, to step down from the ridiculous to the sublime.'

They had reached the boundary fence of Aggrey School and stood under a baobab tree with its leaves rustling overhead like the ceremonial umbrellas of chiefs. Across the golden grass acres stood the school in all its sombre dignity, stable against the ravages of time and generations of schoolboys like the cliff at its feet which withstood the onslaught of the waves.

The two men faced each other, shook hands and went their different ways as if they had met briefly at a foreign airport.

D